"What? This ring? Yes, it was a present from Ryuta. It is rare to find a black pearl as perfect as this, and he told me that he came across it by accident at a jeweler's in Ginza and just couldn't resist buying it. He said he thought it would be perfect for me and I laughed, saying that he probably said that to all the girls, but I never dreamed that I'd be wearing it at his own funeral and so soon. . . ."

Also by Shizuko Natsuki
Published by Ballantine Books:

INNOCENT JOURNEY
MURDER AT MT. FUJI
THE OBITUARY ARRIVES AT TWO O'CLOCK
PORTAL OF THE WIND
THE THIRD LADY

DEATH FROM THE CLOUDS

Shizuko Natsuki

BALLANTINE BOOKS • NEW YORK

Library of Congress Catalog Card Number: 90-93572

ISBN 0-345-36667-0

Printed in Canada

First Edition: April 1991

1

The Phantom in the Sky

I

RYUTA SHIRAFUJI PARKED HIS JAGUAR XJS IN THE PARKING lot of Chofu Airfield. As he looked up at the sky, a satisfied smile played briefly on his lips.

It was 9:30 on the morning of Tuesday, May 12, and the sky was unusually clear for this time of year, just a few wisps of high cirrus clouds. The altitude of the clouds was very important to Ryuta, since a high cloud ceiling is necessary for flying a light aircraft. Although there was a slight breeze, it was nothing to worry about; in fact, Ryuta found himself wishing that the wind were a little stronger: it would have made the flight more interesting.

Chofu Airfield is used mostly by private aircraft, and what with the weather being so unusually good, it was crowded with people eager to get away for the day.

Ryuta headed straight for the met office to check on the weather, because while it might be good at Tokyo, if it were bad over his destination, he would be forced to cancel his flight. He had just reached the door when out stepped a man he had met on several previous occasions. Like Ryuta, he was in his midfifties and was also a company executive.

"Oh, Shirafuji, how's it going?" the man called out in a friendly tone. "I haven't seen you around here for a while."

"Yes, I haven't been up for a couple of months."

"Oh? That's unusual for you—" The man suddenly broke off and his face became solemn. "I *am* sorry, I forgot. I read about your brother in the newspapers; you have my deepest sympathy."

"Thank you."

"It's such a shame, he was still so young."

"Yes, that's why I haven't been able to get over here until now."

"What? You mean that it's been two months since he died?"

"Yes, yesterday was the forty-ninth day, so we held the ashes-burying ceremony. That's why I thought that I'd come over here today, to try and take my mind off it."

"I see. Where are you planning to go?" the man asked.

"I thought I might fly down the north side of Mount Fuji to Nagoya and back," Ryuta replied.

"That sounds nice. I plan to fly north myself, but wherever you go today, the weather is perfect."

Ryuta said good-bye to the man and made his way into the met office. It was a square room with a large weather map on the opposite wall showing the weather at all the main airports in Japan. On the right-hand side of the room a FAX machine received a steady flow of weather reports from the various airports, and a board on the left-hand side showed the VMC (visual meteorological conditions). This last is very important for light aircraft since the majority of them are flown without instruments.

Ryuta checked the conditions in Nagoya, Yao, and Osaka. The weather changes in Japan generally move from west to east, so it is standard practice to check the weather conditions west of one's destination. All three cities were marked

"CAVOK" —meaning that ceiling and visibility were okay and flying conditions were ideal.

Having checked the weather, Ryuta proceeded to submit his flight plan.

It's such a shame, he was still so young.

The other man's words came back to him. His youngest brother, Okito, had been called an ill-fated genius and even, on occasion, an idiot, but on March 24 of this year, shortly after his forty-eighth birthday, he had died a miserable death. He had always been a bit wild, a fact perhaps that explained why he had managed always to look so young. He resembled a poet rather than a scientist, and he deserved to live a much longer, happier life. . . .

Ryuta shook his head to drive such thoughts away.

"It couldn't be helped, he brought it on himself," he muttered, and there was something in his tone that sounded almost defensive.

He submitted his flight plan, putting down his departure time as 10:15, which left him forty-five minutes. He estimated that he would return at 12:15, which would allow him to enjoy a two-hour flight. His plan was approved, and with the formalities out of the way, he made his way to the public telephone near the clubhouse and called his company, which was situated in the main financial district of Marunouchi.

Ryuta Shirafuji was an executive at a computer and office-equipment manufacturer named Ruco, which, despite being a relatively new company, had leaped to the forefront of the industry in the early seventies. It was basically a family business, with Ryuta, at fifty-five, the president, his fifty-two-year-old brother Koji the vice-president, and most of the other executive posts held by relatives.

He spoke to his secretary, and after hearing who had called him that morning, he gave her some instructions before hanging up.

He still had a number of coins left and, for no particular reason, decided to phone someone else. He did not really care who he called, although he did not want to call his wife. He thought of the various girls he knew who worked in the clubs and bars in Ginza or Akasaka, but realized that none of them was likely to be up at this time of the morning, and then his thoughts turned to his niece, Toko Chino.

Her father, Hiroshi Chino, was five years younger than Ryuta; they were cousins, and Hiroshi was one of the directors in the company. Toko was twenty-one years old and a student at a private university in Tokyo. Not having any children himself, Ryuta had always been very fond of her and took her everywhere with him; once, they had even gone on a trip to Hawaii together.

He telephoned her home at Naka-Meguro.

"Hello?"

The phone was answered by a rather husky-sounding woman.

"Is that you, Toko?"

"Oh, hello." She soon recognized his voice.

"Haven't you got any classes today?" he asked.

"No, not until the afternoon."

"Lucky you. What are you doing at the moment?"

"Right now? I just took a shower and washed my hair."

"What, again? You always seem to say that."

"I can't help it, I wash it every day," Toko said.

"Every day? You'll go bald if you're not careful," he warned, bantering.

"Don't worry, we're not all like you, you know."

Ever since Ryuta's hair had started to thin, the subject had been taboo at the office, but Toko did not worry about such touchy subjects with her uncle. For some reason, Ryuta found that he could never get angry with her.

"Are you calling from the office?" she asked.

"No, I, too, won't be going in until this afternoon."

"Where are you then?"

"At Chofu Airfield."

"What, are you going flying again?"

"Again? I haven't been up for two months now and I usually fly at least twice a month, as you well know."

"Yes, nothing has been the same since Okito died, has it?"

Her voice dropped, and Ryuta remembered that she had cried all the way through the funeral. For some reason, this irritated him. She seemed to have had a sort of crush on Okito ever since she was in senior high school, and he could not stop himself from feeling jealous.

"Will you be taking off soon?" she asked.

"Yes."

"I wish you wouldn't go up today."

"Why?"

"Well . . . it's nothing, but I had a dream about Okito last night."

"What kind of dream?" he demanded.

"I saw him standing in a stormy sky with thunderclouds roiling around him." Her voice grew distant as she relived her dream.

"Then what?"

"Oh, that's all really. . . ."

"There's a beautiful clear sky today and very little wind, perfect weather for a flight." Ryuta glanced down at his watch. He had thirty minutes until takeoff. "Well, I must be going now; you never know, I might meet Okito on top of the clouds."

"Please be careful," she said.

"I will, don't worry. Good-bye."

He replaced the receiver and strode off over the tarmac. He still had his preflight checks to run through before he took off. The sun was beating down on him by the time he reached the edge of the runway, and glancing up at the blue sky, he felt a moment of dizziness.

Why had he talked of meeting Okito on top of the clouds like that? He could not understand what had come over him, but strangely, he regretted having spoken so.

II

Chofu Airfield consists of a single eight-hundred-meter runway in the middle of a vast grassy field, which is enclosed with a wire fence. Several houses can be seen beyond the perimeter fence, but there are still several groves of trees that hark back to the time when the area was very rural. Also visible are several two-story concrete buildings left from the time when the area had served as an American base, but these stand empty now, lending a ghost-town-like air to the place.

Ryuta walked through the heat haze over the grass toward the apron where his plane was kept. A large number of planes were standing there at regular intervals, but he did not have much trouble in finding the orange, blue, and white Beechcraft Bonanza with the name RUCO painted on the side. He had owned this plane for almost eighteen years now and was very attached to it.

He stroked the fuselage lovingly for a moment, then opened the door to the cockpit and took out the preflight checklist. He checked the rudder, radio antenna, and flaps, then turned the propeller by hand. The gasoline tanks on a Beechcraft are situated in the wings; the checklist called for him to open the petcock at the bottom of these to drain off any water that might have condensed, but he never bothered to comply with this item. Whenever he returned from a flight, he had the tanks filled to the brim, and thus there was never any danger of water building up in them.

It took him five minutes to finish the external checks and then he climbed aboard and sat down in the pilot's seat. He gripped the joystick and felt the familiar pleasurable rush of excitement this act gave him. He checked the movement of the controls and then cast his eyes over the instruments. Everything seemed to be in order.

"Switches on," he said out loud as he flicked all the switches into the "on" position. He looked over all the instruments again and checked that the gasoline gauge indicated a full tank. He turned on the fuel cock, and then with a final look outside to make sure nobody was standing near the plane, he pressed the starter. He let the engine idle as he waited for the oil temperature to rise, and then he took it up to full power. Putting on the headset, he called the control tower for the latest weather as a way of checking the radio. Everything appeared to be fine.

"This is JA3959, request permission to taxi for takeoff."

The tower replied with instructions and the Ruco company plane started to move. He arrived at the end of the runway just as a Piper made a takeoff.

"JA3959, this is the tower. Runway clear for takeoff."

"Roger, runway clear for takeoff," he replied, and opened the throttle. The engine roared and the whole plane shook as it surged forward. About two-thirds of the way down the runway, it suddenly floated up into the sky. Ryuta continued to climb at 120 knots; given the perfect weather and his eighteen years of experience, it was no wonder that the plane ascended without so much as a quiver.

He could see over the Tama Hills toward the Tanzawa Mountains, and in the distance he glimpsed the waters of Lake Sagami, sparkling in the sunlight. He did not have much time to enjoy the scenery, however. The weather conditions were so good that the sky was full of light aircraft and he had to keep a careful watch to ensure that he did not get too close to any of them. He also had to listen in to their wireless communications.

Five miles from the airfield, he contacted the control tower to report that he would be leaving their jurisdiction; although once having done so, he was free to change his frequency, he preferred to remain on their channel for the time being.

He leveled out at three thousand feet and throttled back to his cruising speed. Although the plane had been shaking slightly with the power of the engine during the ascent, it now settled down. It is said that a plane is smoother than a car, and with the weather as it was, this fact certainly seemed true.

Ryuta was finally able to relax, and settling back in the pilot's seat, he looked out at the scenery. The mountains of Oku-Tama and Oku-Chichibu were clothed in their summer greens, and the cars threading their way along the ribbon of road that wound its way between the peaks looked like tiny beetles. Over to the left Ryuta could see Sagami Bay shining in the morning sun, the freighters and tankers on it no more than tiny dots. Ships, cars, islands—from three thousand feet they all looked so tiny, and although this had been completely predictable, Ryuta still reveled in the sensation. He thought that it was a truly marvelous thing to fly through the air like this, free to go where he chose. Everything on the ground looked so insignificant that he felt he could order things as he wanted them. While this was only an illusion and he knew it, there was a certain arrogance about Ryuta that would allow him almost to believe it while he was flying. He often felt that flying was the ideal hobby for him.

He had taken his private pilot's license eighteen years earlier when he was thirty-seven, and after obtaining a parking space at Chofu Airfield a short while later, he bought the Beechcraft for around ten million yen. Although he had already started the company at that time, it was still a small-scale operation, and a lot of people at the time criticized him behind his back for being too extravagant. However, owning an aircraft is not as expensive as most people think. After the initial purchase and registration, it only costs about one hundred thousand yen per month for maintenance and the annual checkup, and a further five hundred thousand for insurance. There is a nominal fee for parking at the airfield and, of course, the price of fuel every time it is taken up for a flight, but Ryuta, unlike most people, believed flying was probably a cheaper hobby than driving expensive cars or sailing. Not that he needed to worry about such things anymore; given the size of his company, the costs were negligible. His Beechcraft was getting a bit old, but he was very attached to it; although he intended to continue flying it for some time to come, he was considering buying a second, more agile aircraft.

When he thought back on the way that Ruco had expanded since its founding in 1967—especially after 1974, when the revolutionary miniature calculator, the "SuperMini," had been introduced—even he could hardly believe it. In 1975 they had built the modern new factory in Yokosuka, and the following year, work on the new fifteen-story head office in the Marunouchi district was completed. It was strange to think that only twenty years had passed since they had been working out of a back-street factory, employing a mere thirty people.

The company owed it all to his genius of a brother, Okito, and his incredible inventions. . . .

Ryuta quickly broke off this train of thought as an image of Okito's thin, aesthetic face, with its intelligent eyes and pointed chin, flashed before his eyes. He hurriedly dismissed the vision.

His death was unavoidable.

He tightened his grip on the stick and turned the nose of the aircraft slightly toward the southwest.

At that moment a huge black thunderhead appeared before him, a wind whipping at its edges.

That can't be! Ryuta thought incredulously, and instinctively thrust the control column to one side to avoid it. However, the cloud vanished as suddenly as it had appeared—it had been nothing but an illusion—and now the sky was again clear. It was some time before his pulse returned to normal.

Why on earth did I imagine something like that? It's not like me. . . . He suddenly remembered what Toko had said to him on the phone just before he took off. *I saw him standing in a stormy sky with thunderclouds roiling around him.* He could hear her saying it, and then he remembered his reply. *You never know, I might meet Okito up there above the clouds.*

He had a chilling premonition, and then the next minute the engine started to stutter. Before he could think of doing anything about it, it stopped altogether.

He reached out for the booster switch and tried to restart it, but it just misfired and would not start. He tried it once, twice, three times, but it was no good, the engine would not come back to life! He felt a needle of pain in his chest and a chill ran through his body.

"Mayday . . . Mayday!" He sent out a distress call without realizing what he was doing. "This is JA3959, my engine has stalled," he said in Japanese; this was no time to try and think about English.

"What is your position, JA3959?" the control tower asked calmly.

"I am approximately twenty-five miles southwest of Chofu."

"Scope one-two-zero-zero, identify."

The controller seemed to be speaking far too slowly, and while this was probably done in an effort to calm him down, it had the opposite effect, and Ryuta started to panic. However, he did manage to press the button he was instructed to and he knew that this would cause his position to blink on the radar screen at the airport. He tried the booster again.

"It's no good, it won't start! It must be condensation!"

"In that case, please prepare yourself for an emergency landing. Remain calm and look for a suitable site."

That was right, when the engine stopped, he was supposed to go into a glide, keep the nose up, and control the descent. He had never had to make an emergency landing before, but it was not as if he was a novice at flying; he should be able to manage it . . . he had to!

He pulled the nose up until it was at about forty-five degrees. Without the engine to power it, the plane was unable to stay in the air; all Ryuta could do was try to find a spot to make an emergency landing—but there was nothing below him but mountains!

No, wait a minute, wasn't that a lake over there? That's right, he should be near the string of lakes that border Mount Fuji's northern side . . . yes, he could make out Lake Yamanaka ahead of him.

"This is JA3959, I am going to attempt an emergency landing in Lake Yamanaka."

The trees and lake seemed to rush up to meet him. He was helpless to control his approach any longer. The lake filled his vision now, and at the bottom, in the dark depths, he thought he could see Okito's face, waiting for him.

III

    The Beechcraft crashed into Lake Yamanaka near the northern shore at 10:32 in the morning of Tuesday, May 12.
    The chief of the Five Lakes police station and four of his men were the first to arrive at the scene, but there had been several witnesses to the accident. Although it was a weekday, there were numerous boats out on the lake, filled with anglers who had come to enjoy a day's fishing; a number of them had seen the plane fly in from the northeast and crash into the lake.
    One of them had rushed up to the phone at the bus stop and called the police. The police station is situated fairly close to Lake Yamanaka, so they had all heard the sound of the impact and had been wondering what had happened when the phone call came through.
    While five of the officers hurried to the scene of the accident, those that remained in the station contacted the prefectural headquarters to let them know what had happened. They were still on the line when word came in to headquarters from Chofu Airfield that a Beechcraft, number JA3959, which had taken off earlier that day, had contacted their tower to say that its engine had stalled and the pilot was going to attempt an emergency landing in Lake Yamanaka. Since then, they had heard no more from the plane and, fearing the worst, had called to request an urgent search be made of the area for any wreckage. Headquarters said they would send a special squad out to deal with the crash and asked the men at the Five Lakes station to see if they could manage to rescue the pilot and any casualties from the crash.
    The chief of the Five Lakes station was forty-five-year-old Superintendent Ukyo Nakazato; five years earlier, it had been he who had solved the case of the Asahi Hills murder. It had been a very complicated case involving a major pharmaceutical company and the machinations among the members of the family that ran it. So successful had Detective Nakazato been in solving the case that he was put in charge of the plainclothes division at a much larger police station; three

years later he was promoted to the rank of superintendent and given command of his old station back at Five Lakes.

The plane had crashed about twenty yards from the end of a small promontory jutting out into the lake. The water was quite shallow at this point and part of the wreckage was sticking up out of its surface. One of the wings with its orange mark on a white background had been flung into a small grove of trees nearby and other small pieces of wreckage lay scattered around the area, but the bulk of it appeared to have sunk beneath the waters of the lake.

When Nakazato arrived, a crowd of about thirty people had already gathered to look at the wreck, but luckily none of them had been hurt in the crash.

"Hey, there's someone in there!" he cried, peering at the part of the wreckage that was visible above the water. "Quickly, get a boat and we'll try and rescue them!"

He and two of his men jumped into a motorboat that was moored nearby and hurried over to the remains of the downed plane. The cockpit had been caught on a large boulder, which kept it above the water, and they could make out a middle-aged man still strapped into the pilot's seat. His eyes were closed, but his face showed very little sign of injury.

The three policemen tried without success to open the cockpit door, then tried instead to pull the man out through one of the smashed windows. He appeared to be dead. As Nakazato cradled the victim's head and body in his arms and as they struggled with his inert form, his lips moved a fraction.

"Okito . . . Okito . . ."

At least, that is what Nakazato thought he said.

At Nakazato's request, the fire brigade and self-defense corps arrived to seal off the crash site. At the same time, the authorities at Chofu Airfield got in touch with the Ministry of Transport's Aviation Authorities at Haneda Airport and informed them of the crash. The Aviation Authority in turn contacted the Crash Investigation Committee and asked them to dispatch a team of investigators to the scene. The team was chosen from among veteran pilots, air-traffic controllers, and other experts on aviation; one of its members set out for the site of the crash within the hour. His job was to work with the local police to learn as much as possible about the crash and to instruct them on procedures.

When the investigation team from prefectural headquarters arrived, about an hour after the crash, they found that Nakazato had succeeded in removing the pilot from the cockpit of the plane and had laid him on a sheet in the shade of a pine tree near the lakeshore.

After whispering Okito's name faintly as he was lifted out of the plane, Ryuta passed into unconsciousness, and by the time they had managed to get him to the shore, he had ceased breathing. A medical expert who had accompanied the team from headquarters examined the body and pronounced him dead.

"Although the head seems to be undamaged, there are signs of heavy internal bleeding. It's a miracle he was still conscious at all when you got to him."

The officers who were standing nearby all sighed when they heard this. They could not understand why anyone would want to do something as dangerous as flying for mere pleasure and felt that he had brought his death on himself.

"Was the pilot the only one on board?" Nakazato asked, looking over at the head of the team, Superintendent Tsurumi.

"Yes, the president of the Ruco Corporation, Ryuta Shirafuji, fifty-five years old, with a flying history of eighteen years."

Tsurumi had checked with Chofu Airfield before departing and had been able to gather some information about the plane. After he had spoken, he nodded to Nakazato in a friendly fashion.

Five years earlier, Tsurumi had headed the investigation team that had been sent from headquarters to investigate the death of Yohei Wada, the chairman of Wada Pharmaceuticals, whose body had been found at his holiday villa during the New Year's holidays. The two of them had worked together on, and finally, succeeded in solving, the case that later became famous as "The Murder at Mount Fuji." At the time Tsurumi had been an inspector in the homicide squad, but since then had been promoted to superintendent. Once again, he was heading an investigative team.

"I hear that he was in touch with Chofu Airfield until the moment he crashed."

"Yes, that's why we were able to pinpoint the crash so easily, although there's no shortage of witnesses." Tsurumi was a very impatient man and tended to speak rather fast. "Yes," he now said, "but what on earth do you think could have caused the crash; the weather is perfect today." Nakazato gazed up at Mount Fuji, which stood out against the clear blue sky, while Nakazato replied.

"He told the control tower that his engine had stopped and that he was unable to restart it." Tsurumi said. "He said that he thought it might be due to condensation in the fuel tank and that he was going to try and make a forced landing in the lake. Obviously, he wasn't successful. Judging from the way that the nose is pointing up out of the water, he came in tail-first."

From the way he was speaking, it was obvious that Tsurumi thought Nakazato knew nothing about aircraft, but this was not in fact the case. One of his old friends from high school, who was now working as a gynecologist in the Mitaka area of Tokyo, owned a light aircraft, which he used to visit patients in remote areas. He had been doing this for ten years now, flying out to Oshima and other islands off Tokyo and bringing back dangerously ill patients for treatment in one of the major hospitals.

Nakazato had accompanied him on one of his less urgent trips, but there had been a lot of turbulence that day, and although Nakazato had tried to remain outwardly calm, he swore to himself that he would never do it again.

"What do you mean by 'condensation in the fuel tank'?" he now asked.

"He must have neglected to open the petcock on the fuel tank under the wing to drain off any buildup of condensation." Airplane crashes fell under the jurisdiction of the second investigation team, and despite their relative rarity, Tsurumi had obviously studied up on the subject.

"But surely opening the petcock on the fuel tanks is one of the basic preflight checks."

"Yes, but you'd be surprised to hear how many people fail to do it. There are a large number of veterans, especially those happy-go-lucky types, who always make a point of filling the gasoline tanks on their planes as soon as they land and think that that is sufficient to solve the problem."

The main fuel tank on an aircraft is situated in the wings, and if the tank is not full when a sudden drop in temperature occurs, the moisture will condense out of the air trapped in the tank. Water, being heavier than gasoline, collects at the bottom and can easily be drained off by the pilot before he starts his flight. If, however, it gets drawn into the engine, it will settle on the spark plug, causing the engine to stall, and once the plug is wet, it is very difficult to get the engine to start again.

When Nakazato had gone flying with his gynecologist friend, he had asked questions about everything, and he remembered being given an explanation about condensation. Although a naturally inquisitive person, he had felt at the time that if he knew just what was going on, he would cease being so scared during the flight.

"But surely Mr. Shirafuji would have checked to see if his tanks were full or not before he took off."

"Yes, I agree."

"But then how could any condensation have taken place?" Nakazato persisted.

"I don't know; we'll have to wait for the experts to give us their opinion later." Tsurumi looked away from his men, who were still searching the scene. "If you ask me, though, I'd say that when the tanks were filled, they probably left a small gap above the level of gasoline, and that was sufficient to allow condensation to take place. When Shirafuji prepared to make his flight, he probably looked at the fuel gauge and, seeing that it was more or less full, didn't bother to check properly.

"He knew that he had not done all his checks, though, and that's why he guessed that it must've been condensation when his engine gave out on him," Tsurumi concluded.

"I suppose it all depends on whether or not he made a habit of filling his tanks immediately after each flight," Nakazato said thoughtfully. "When was his last flight prior to this one?"

"I'm afraid that I haven't heard yet, but I should think it must have been more than a month ago. After that incident . . ."

"Yes, I quite agree." Nakazato nodded. He was only five feet six inches tall, overweight, and his head looked too large for his body. "Okito Shirafuji did more than anyone to make the Ruco Corporation what it is today, and after he died the way he did, his brother could hardly go up for a joyride in his plane. No, I think that it's likely that this is the first time he has used the plane since his brother's death."

He looked out at the plane's wreckage, sticking up out of the surface of the lake, almost dazzling in the bright afternoon sun. The police had to deal with the body, but the investigation of the aircraft would be left to the team of specialists when they arrived. The police had other things to do.

But what if there was something suspicious about the circumstances surrounding the crash? he suddenly wondered.

He brushed the thought aside as soon as it occurred. He realized that it was probably the sight of the familiar white wall shining in the sunlight amid the holiday villas on the opposite side of the lake at Asahi Hills that had made him think of it.

IV

"Toko . . . Toko!"

Toko Chino was standing in front of the notice board outside the university offices when she heard her name called, and swinging around on her heel, she saw Akira Takubo's slim silhouette hurrying down the gloomy corridor. He was wearing a light green sport shirt and jeans and carrying two or three thin exercise books in his hand as he made his way toward her, scuffing his feet as he came. When he reached her, he took a breath before he spoke.

"How's it going . . . it must have been very hard for you," he said, frowning. He knew that one of her relatives had died during the spring vacation. "I haven't seen you at all this term; have you been coming?"

"Yes, but you were never here when I came."

"Really? I suppose I must have been working on those days."

Toko and Akira were both in their third year at a private university in the Chiyoda area of central Tokyo, but Toko was studying French literature while Akira's major was commercial science. Toko had matriculated straight from high school and was thus only twenty-one, but it had taken Akira an extra year to pass the entrance exam and so he was a year older. However, they had both attended the same general culture course for the first two years and still saw quite a lot of each other; indeed, it was generally assumed that they were going steady.

"Oh, literary history has been canceled for today," she said, looking up at the board.

"Really?" Akira said, and looked down at his watch. Toko also glanced down at her own watch; it was almost 12:50. After Ryuta had called her that morning, she made herself some brunch, and by the time she was ready to leave for classes, it was almost twelve o'clock.

"Let's go out somewhere," Akira suggested.

"What about your classes, Akira?"

"Don't worry about them, there's nothing important. How about you?"

"No, okay, let's go."

With that, the two of them started to walk toward the entrance of the building. Toko was five-four and Akira was about six inches taller and quite slim. He could almost be described as handsome, but there was something about him that spoiled the image. Maybe it was the strange way he had of bending his legs slightly as he walked, giving him a rather peculiar, bouncing gait, or then again, it might have been his clothes, which, while not being in thoroughly bad taste, did not quite suit him. It was probably not any one thing that spoiled his looks, but a variety of small things combined.

His parents were farmers and Toko sometimes wondered if he walked the way he did because he had been used to helping out in the fields as a young boy, but she never put her thoughts into words since she did not want to hurt his feelings.

"Have you had your lunch yet?" he asked.

"Yes, I had something before I left home, how about you?"

"Mmm . . ." he replied, apparently meaning that he had eaten, too.

They walked to the parking lot at the edge of the campus, where he had left his yellow Mirage. The car was quite old now and the paint was starting to peel off in places.

Whenever he suggested that they go for a drive, he usually headed for the country. Toko guessed this was because he was happier out of the crowded city. She was not sure whether she preferred the city or not, but she was quite happy to go along with him when they were cutting classes.

"Where shall we go?" she asked.

"How about Disneyland?"

This was the last place she had expected him to suggest. They had gone there about ten months earlier, with another couple, but since it had been a Saturday, the place had been very crowded. Akira did not seem to have enjoyed it very much and had never mentioned it since.

"Yes, let's!" Toko exclaimed happily. She was really rather partial to that kind of amusement park.

They drove out of the college grounds and up onto the expressway at the Nishi-Kanda ramp. The traffic moved along quite smoothly until they reached the central loop, which was jammed bumper to bumper, but, as usual, Akira did not seem to be irritated by the delay.

"I called you two or three times but you were out, so I didn't try again," he said hesitantly, after they had been sitting in silence for a while. "I guessed that you must have been very busy."

"When was this?"

"The day after the newspapers carried the story about Okito Shirafuji's death."

"Oh, in that case, I would have been at his house in Egota for the wake."

An autopsy had been performed on Okito's body, so the wake had been delayed twenty-four hours.

They drove on in silence for a while. The best thing about their relationship was that they were able to discuss things quite openly and so, at the moment, they both felt very awkward at not being able to continue. Toko guessed that Akira was not sure whether it would hurt her to talk about the death in her family or whether it would help.

"It said in the papers that he died of natural causes, but I cannot help feeling that he really committed suicide."

It was Toko who had started talking again. She felt that it would make her feel better if she were to discuss everything with him.

"Suicide?" Akira repeated, although he did not seem to be very surprised. There had already been rumors to that effect in some of the papers, and she guessed that he must have read them. "Do you mean that you think he might have taken more sleeping pills than usual?" he asked.

"Yes, he drank too much and took sleeping pills regularly, so his heart was very weak. That day he took more than usual, although it was not in itself a fatal dose, but nobody knows for sure how much he usually took, and apparently they were not able to find out from the autopsy."

"Did he leave a note?"

"No, there was nothing like that."

Okito Shirafuji had lived alone in a house at Egota and his body was discovered on the morning of March 26. He had a cleaning lady who came in every other day, and when she found him lying in his bed, his body was already quite cold. It was she who telephoned the police.

The subsequent investigation discovered that Okito had been dead for approximately thirty hours before he was discovered, which would mean that he died on the night of the twenty-fourth. The autopsy discovered a large quantity of barbiturates in his bloodstream.

In the weeks before his death, he had appeared only occasionally at the laboratories in Nishi-Oizumi and very seldom went to the head office in the Marunouchi district. Several people close to him said that he had seemed to be spending most of his time drinking and taking barbiturates and that he was a wreck both physically and mentally.

The police decided that he had died from a heart attack brought on by habitual use of sleeping pills and put it down to death by natural causes. However, the rumors that he had committed suicide soon started to spread through the Ruco offices, and it was not long before the press got wind of them.

In the late sixties and early seventies when he was being acclaimed as a genius inventor, Okita had acquired a wide knowledge of many things, not just relating to his specialty, electronics, but to medicine and pharmacology as well. Since then, he had lived a very wild life, but while he may have been wrecking his body, he had the knowledge to tell just how badly he was hurting himself. He would have been able to calculate just how much more alcohol and barbiturates it would take to kill him and could easily have chosen that way out. His lonely death might well have been suicide, but he was able to do it in such a way that it could never be proved, or so the rumors went.

"When I first got to know you, I read a bit about the Ruco Corporation, and although I don't know very much, all the reports agreed that the company's tremendous growth was due solely to Okito's research and development."

"Yes, I think that's probably true."

"Then why should a man so important to the company be allowed to die a lonely death like that?"

The car finally managed to break out of the jam and entered the Bay Road. Beneath the graceful curve of the elevated expressway, the reclaimed land was packed with tiny little houses. The sea was a dazzling, silver mirror under the clear blue sky and the factories on the opposite shore were pouring white smoke out of their tall chimneys. It was as if the total energy of the city had been captured in a single picture.

Toko dropped her eyes to her hands and mourned Okito's death anew. She looked up slowly to tell Akira about it when she suddenly saw a huge black thunderhead appear in the blue sky ahead of them. She gasped in surprise and looked again, but it had vanished.

It had just been her imagination, no more than an illusion, but it served to remind her of her dream the previous night. In her dream there had been a gigantic cloud towering up into the sky, just like the one she thought she had just seen, and there in the storm-racked sky had stood Okito. His thin figure, his hair whipping about his well-defined features, was very dear to her.

"Okito!" she had cried out to him as loudly as she could, and he had answered her, a strange smile playing over his features.

"Watch me, Toko. I've got a present for all of them."

"A present?"

"Yes . . ."

For some reason, she had not been able to tell Ryuta this part of her dream when she had spoken to him on the phone earlier that morning. The vision of Okito in her dream had finished with these words:

"I will send them all death from here on top of the clouds."

2

The Sand Castle

I

"THE RUCO CORPORATION CAN BE SAID TO HAVE BEEN started in 1947 by Ryuta's father, although in those days it was only a small company called Shirafuji Manufacturing Corporation."

Toko had started to tell Akira the whole history of the company as they drove along the Bay Road.

"Oh, yes, I remember reading something about that. It was a small machine shop that employed about thirty people, wasn't it?"

"Yes, that's right. When it first started, Ryuta was still in senior high school, Uncle Koji and my father were in junior high, and Okito was in elementary school."

Over the next ten years or so, Shirafuji Manufacturing Corporation had had its ups and downs but did not change very much. Ryuta, Koji, and their cousin Hiroshi, Toko's father, all graduated from college and found jobs in different companies, Koji taking a job in a bank despite having ma-

22

jored in science. Okito was the only one who had chosen a different course, and after graduating with a degree in electronic engineering, he stayed on at the university as an assistant and taught electrical-theory classes. However, he did not get along very well with the other assistants or with the professors and left after about a year to join his father's company, where he started doing his own research.

This had all happened in 1964, when he was twenty-five years old. He was totally absorbed with his research and unable to get along with other people. He had always been a lonely, stubborn man, and it was around this time that this side of his character had come to the fore.

He was very interested in calculators and locked himself away in his laboratory for days on end while he tried to realize his ideas. The following year—1965—he produced the world's first office computer and followed this the next year with a transistorized, programmable, desktop calculator.

This was when talk about forming a company to bring his products to the market first began, and his father and two brothers decided to close down the Shirafuji Manufacturing Corporation and start a new corporation, which they called Ruco. Ryuta was now thirty-five and Koji thirty-two, but they both resigned their jobs to become, respectively, president and vice-president of the new company. Their father, who was now getting rather elderly and was not in very good health, and Okito, who was not very interested in the actual running of the company, were both given the title of managing director.

"The name Ruco is a combination of 'Ru' for Ryuta a 'C' for Koji and the 'O' for Okito," Toko continued.

"I see, and when did your father join the company?" Akira asked as he drove the yellow Mirage eastward.

"I'm pretty certain that it was in 1970; I was still only four years old at the time. He worked in the research labs of another electrical company until then, but Ruco was growing at a terrific pace and Ryuta wanted to keep management within the family as much as possible, so he was asked to join."

"That would be about the time that Okito was at his peak, wasn't it?" Akira asked. "Everyone said that he was one of the leading geniuses in the country."

"Yes, he was bringing out several new products every year, but the most famous has to be the SuperMini."

Okito had invented the world's first personal calculator in 1973, and in 1974 it was marketed as the SuperMini. An instant success, it won acclaim throughout the world.

Until then, people had thought of calculators solely as office machines, and the calculator of the sixties was about the same size as a personal computer today. The introduction of transistors meant that these machines shrank to about the size of a telephone, but they remained very much tied to the office, and even in the electronics industry, nobody thought it possible to make them small enough to become portable.

Okito's revolutionary idea had not only been to make one small enough to be portable, but to make one that would be simple enough for anyone to use without any effort. By using integrated circuitry that had been developed by American military and space programs, he finally succeeded in producing a revolutionary compact calculator.

Although the SuperMini used existing technology and could not really be called an invention, it represented a giant step forward in the miniaturization of electronics and it was marketed at a remarkably low price. The first commercially manufactured calculator had sold in 1964 for five hundred thousand yen, and although the price dropped regularly with every subsequent new product, in the spring of 1972, the average price was still around fifty thousand yen. When the SuperMini was first introduced, however, it was marketed at the unbelievably low price of twelve thousand yen, and the reaction from the public both in Japan and overseas was so favorable that even the staff of Ruco had been taken by surprise.

Ryuta and Koji realized that they could not afford to waste this opportunity and they put everything they had into an export drive while running a PR campaign on Japanese television. Luck seemed to be with them and everything they did turned out successfully, so much so that their sales figures for the year ending in March 1975 were up an amazing sixty percent over the preceding year. The company continued to grow at an astounding rate after that and soon became one of the most active and sought-after stocks on the Tokyo exchange.

"Strangely enough, however," Toko continued, "no sooner did they start to build the new factory and offices and increase the work force than Uncle Okito's position in the company deteriorated dramatically."

Akira looked puzzled. "What do you mean? He made lots of new inventions or products after that, didn't he?"

"Yes, but I remember my father saying—I think it was when I was in senior high school—that Uncle Okito seemed to have lost interest in calculators after he perfected the SuperMini. I suppose he felt he'd exhausted that field. He had trained several very promising young technicians in the lab, and I think that most of the products after that were due mainly to their labors, but Okito, being the most famous, was credited with having produced them."

"Yes, well, they say that scholars and artists are only really creative for a limited time," Akira offered.

"That's true. And that's why I think it might've been better if he had just retired then and spent the rest of his life enjoying himself, seeing the world or flying his own plane like Uncle Ryuta."

Peering out at the sky through the windshield, she remembered how happy Ryuta had sounded when he had called her from the airfield that morning. It was a beautiful sunny day and the blue sky was so bright that it made her eyes sting, but no matter how she searched, there was no sign of the Ruco plane anywhere. The sea on their right shone like burnished metal as it reflected the midday sun.

They crossed the bridge over the Arakawa River and approached Urayasu where Tokyo Disneyland is situated.

"What did he work on after he finished with calculators?" Akira asked hesitantly. The company had made it a point never to discuss Okito's private life or research, and he wondered if Toko would mind him asking.

"I heard that he was working on something completely new, something to do with energy, but I don't know anything about it really. Apparently he wanted to create a new source of power that would be smaller and more powerful than anything ever dreamed of before. Something the size of an ordinary flashlight battery that would provide enough power for an entire household's needs for about twenty years. If he had succeeded, it would have changed society dramatically, and I have no doubt that he'd have been awarded the Nobel Prize."

"As small and as powerful as possible . . ." Akira reflected aloud. "It's the same concept as the SuperMini."

"Why yes, so it is. But his research cost a vast amount of money. He built a huge factory and filled it with apparatus to analyze chemical compounds and compress them to their smallest possible size. He built all kinds of apparatus and stuck with his dream for the last ten years."

"Did he have any success?"

"I don't know, but I think that his funds ran out before he got that far."

Okito had started work on the project in the late seventies, and in the beginning Ryuta and Koji were more than happy to finance it, writing off the costs as research and development. After all, Ruco had only gotten where it was because of Okito's research, and there was a good chance that he might come up with another successful product like the SuperMini, so they simply sat back and waited expectantly for his results.

However, things did not go as smoothly as they had hoped, and five years later, Okito still had not made the necessary breakthrough. Meanwhile his research costs escalated alarmingly. To make matters worse, as time passed, the negative side of his personality surfaced more and more, and his assistants, who had long admired him as a scientist, found they could no longer work with a man who would not listen to their advice and who ruled his laboratory like a dictator, so one by one they drifted away. In the end, he was left all alone in the huge research laboratory he had built in Nishi-Oizumi in northern Tokyo.

Two years ago the expenses for the laboratory had come to over one billion yen, but Okito had asked for still more money in order to make an experiment. Ryuta had called a board meeting, and although the members of the board agreed to give him the money, they had insisted that he leave them his shares in the company as collateral. By this stipulation, they were saying that Okito had to keep his research within certain limits, and if this was not satisfactory to him, the company would only give him the money in the form of a loan.

Okito could not have cared less about any conditions they imposed so long as he was able to get his new equipment. All he could think about was the experiment, and he felt sure that this time he would succeed.

Unfortunately, the equipment on which he had spent over two hundred million yen did not prove to be the key he was looking for and he found himself back at square one. By now he was in his late forties and had probably reached his peak as a researcher.

When Toko thought of this, her heart ached with sadness for him.

"It was a little before that," she remembered, "yes, about three years ago that he started to drink more and take barbiturates regularly. He lived alone in his house at Egota and there was nobody close to him to warn him about what he was doing to himself."

"What about his wife?"

"He married very young—when he was still a student— to an older woman and their son was born soon afterward. Ryuta once told me that he had been forced to marry her because of the child, but about ten years later, she became ill and died. He never married again, but apparently he had a lot of women. He never did anything by halves, and people say that outside the laboratory his life was a shambles, but I prefer to think that he was just more honest about himself

than most of us are.'' Although Toko did not quite realize it
herself, she had always felt very protective toward him.

"What happened to his child?" Akira asked.

"After his wife died, Okito's mother looked after him.
Both my grandmother and grandfather are dead now, but
Akihito—that's his son's name—graduated from junior high
school while they were still alive, and went to study in the
States. He still lives abroad somewhere; I haven't seen him
for at least ten years now.''

"But surely, when Okito died . . ." Akira began.

"Yes, of course we tried to get in touch with him, but he
was away on a trip somewhere and nobody knew how to
contact him. He didn't even manage to get back in time for
the funeral.''

Apparently Akihito had returned a few days after the funeral, but Toko had not seen him yet. She guessed that Okito
must have wanted to see his son again before he died, and
thinking of her uncle's sensitive face, and the miserable,
lonely death he suffered, she had to bite her lip to hold back
the tears she felt building behind her eyes.

After he had given the company all his stock to cover the
cost of the research funds, he had asked for several more
grants, but each time he was turned down.

As he could not proceed with his research, and with his
private life a shambles, Okito seldom even bothered to visit
his laboratory anymore. He would occasionally turn up at
the head office, but people there started to shun him quite
openly. Finally, he was demoted from the position of managing director to that of adviser.

Ryuta and Koji had warned him several times about the
direction his career was heading; they told him that he should
hand over control of his laboratory to the company and go
work with the other research staff in their research facility in
Kurihama, but he would not listen. Eventually, they just gave
up trying to help and felt that whatever happened to him was
no more or less than he deserved.

"It's not as if Uncle Ryuta is a cold person," Toko explained, "it's just that as the president of a major corpora-

tion, a lot of responsibility rests on his shoulders, and I think that he just couldn't find the time to worry about Okito any longer. My father says—''

The thought that perhaps she should not be saying all this to someone outside the family caused her to break off in midsentence, but she could not keep any secrets from Akira and immediately picked up the thread of her story.

''My father was only his cousin, and he was only two years older than Okito; I think maybe he was the closest to him and worried more than the others.''

Hiroshi was one of the executives of the company, but he was a quiet man, a technician more than a businessman, and never held any opinions about the running of the company, preferring to leave that side of things to Ryuta. However, he could not bear to see what was happening to Okito and pleaded with Ryuta and Koji several times to do something about it. He also went to Okito's house to try to discuss the matter with him.

''It was no good, though; in the end, he couldn't do anything.''

''It's a shame, but I'm sure that Okito must have realized how he felt,'' Akira offered.

''I don't know . . .''

''What?''

''To tell the truth, I sometimes think that Okito must have died hating the company.''

Akira looked surprised and did not speak for a few moments. Then he said, ''Why do you say that?''

''It's just a feeling I have and . . . I had a strange dream last night.''

Once again she could see Okito standing in the midst of the swirling black clouds, and she was just about to tell Okito about it when she suddenly changed her mind. A fearful premonition blew through her like a cold wind.

She looked out through the windshield again at the sky; it was still as blue as ever, with just a wisp of white cirrus in the distance.

''Let's talk about something else,'' she said.

She reached out and turned on the radio. It was tuned to an FM station that was broadcasting a news and music program. She heard a couple of well-known personalities chatting when suddenly there was a pause.

"A piece of news has just come into the studio," one of them said in a rather tense voice. "At 11:30 this morning, a Beechcraft light airplane crashed into Lake Yamanaka and the pilot, the only person on board, was fatally injured. The deceased was Ryuta Shirafuji, age fifty-five, president of the Ruco Corporation . . ."

II

Toko and Akira were almost at the Urayasu interchange when they heard the news, and after hurrying off the expressway, Toko rushed to a pay phone to call her home. Luckily, her mother, Sachiko, was there, but she knew even less about the accident than Toko.

"Are you sure you didn't make a mistake?" she asked. "You must have misheard them." Her mother sounded very calm and seemed unwilling to take the news seriously.

"No, they said quite clearly, 'Ryuta Shirafuji, president of the Ruco Corporation.' " Even as she spoke, however, Toko prayed that she was wrong. "Anyway, I'll call the office and Uncle Ryuta's house and then call you back when I've got some more information."

She hurriedly hung up and dialed the company, then Ryuta's home in Nishi-Ogikubo, but both lines were busy. She called home again, and by this time her mother had also begun to worry.

"The best thing for you to do is to come back here," she said. "If something's happened, I'm sure that your father will get in touch."

Toko and Akira hurried back down the Bay Road in the direction they had just come from, but when they hit the city, traffic was still jammed solid, and it was three o'clock by the time she arrived home.

"It seems to be one thing after the other, so be careful now, you hear?" Akira said.

"Yes, I'll call you," Toko promised, and waved to him as she hurried up the path to the house. Sachiko, looking very pale, met her at the door.

"I just heard the story on the television and I also had a call from your father. There seems to be no doubt, it was Ryuta's plane that crashed into Lake Yamanaka."

"But . . . but . . . what about uncle?" Toko spluttered.

"We still don't know anything for certain," Sachiko replied, as if denying the truth could undo the fact.

"I'm going to the house in Nishi-Ogikubo. If there's any news, we'll hear it there first," Toko said.

"That's true, but I think I'll stay here a little longer and see what happens." Then as Toko started toward the front door again, Sachiko called out, "You're not going to go dressed like that, are you?"

Toko was wearing a red checked blouse and a white mini-skirt and was still carrying her schoolbooks in a large shoulder bag. Sachiko looked at her in dismay.

"You should at least put on something a little less flamboyant," she said.

Although Sachiko was usually very easygoing, she sometimes amazed Toko with her practicality. Toko changed into a cream blouse and black skirt, then Sachiko drove her down to Meguro Station.

Toko took a train to Ogikubo Station and then a taxi to Ryuta's house. It was much quicker that way than if she had taken a cab the whole way, but even so, it was 4:30 by the time she arrived.

The house was set in the middle of a large lawn and took up a whole block in an expensive residential area near the Zenpukuji pond. As Ryuta and his wife were childless, the house was quite small, considering the amount of land it was set on. It had turquoise Spanish tiles on the roof, cream walls, and a turret in one corner. Looking at it for the first time, the name "Blue Chateau," sprang immediately to mind. It was surrounded by a simple metal fence with a climbing rose growing over it and it was very open—as, indeed, was Ryuta himself.

As she left the taxi in front of the main gate Toko felt a momentary wave of nostalgia wash over her. Ryuta and her father had brought her here to play countless times when she was a child, but beginning around the time she entered senior high school, her uncle had not asked her over so often, preferring instead to take her out to Ginza, Karuizawa, and sometimes even as far as Hawaii.

The lilacs in the garden were in full bloom and four cars were parked haphazardly outside the front of the house. They had obviously been left in great haste and bore silent testimony to the suddenness of the tragedy that had overtaken the household.

As Toko hurried toward the house she uttered a small cry of pain when her eye fell on a small circular lawn and sand pit on the opposite side of the drive. About the time that Toko was born, Ryuta had been an avid golfer, and these were the remains of the practice green and bunker he had had constructed in the garden. He was a perfectionist at everything he turned his hand to and he had persevered with his game until he managed to get his handicap down to three. Next, he had become absorbed in flying, and with neglect, the green had become overgrown until it was just another grassy plot, but it had provided Toko with the perfect playground when she was young.

She recalled one day when she was still in nursery school— she must have been three or four years old—Ryuta had brought her here and she was playing in the sand pit when Okito had appeared with a boy who was six or seven years older than she. Okito had gone into the house, but the boy had obviously been told to play with her since he climbed reluctantly into the sand pit.

He squatted down next to her and started to help her build a castle. Being older, he was much more adept at it than she was, and soon he had built a gateway with towers on it. Toko was thrilled and gathered sand for him as diligently as she could. As soon as the castle was on the verge of completion, however, he suddenly knocked it down with his hand. It was almost as if he had planned to do this from the beginning; he knocked down the castle he had gone to so much trouble to build, then stood up and strode into the house. Toko had burst into tears, but the boy did not so much as glance at her.

Even now she could picture the boy's figure, straight-backed and with long, thin legs protruding from his shorts.

The boy had been Okito's only son, Akihito, and after that day, Toko had met him several times at family get-togethers. Although he could be quite nice to her, he was sometimes very cruel. Despite this, however, she liked him and followed him around like a faithful dog. Their relationship was not to last, though, because when she was still only seven or eight, Akihito had left for school in the States and she never saw him again.

The scene that had taken place in the sand pit all those years ago briefly flashed before her eyes before disappearing again. She had probably remembered it because this was the first time she had come to Ryuta's house in such a long time and subconsciously she wanted to turn her back on a painful reality.

She strode up to the bronze-covered front door and was standing there wondering whether she should ring the bell or just go in quietly so as not to disturb the occupants when suddenly the door opened and her father, Hiroshi, hurried out.

"Oh, Dad!" she cried.

"Toko . . ."

Hiroshi, who would be fifty this year, was of medium height and weight, and his graying hair was neatly parted. He looked down compassionately at his daughter and asked, "Have you heard the news?"

"Yes, that's why . . . but . . . what about Uncle Ryuta?"

Hiroshi frowned and shook his head. "I'm afraid it's true. Koji has gone down to the site and the body will probably be brought back here late tonight or early to-morrow morning."

Toko was at a loss for words.

"I have to get back to the office now," her father went on. "Apparently there's been a ceaseless stream of inquiries and the newspapers are anxious to get a statement. I should be back later, but in the meantime, I'd be grateful if you could try to help your aunt Hisako."

Toko stood dumbly and watched as her father backed his Toyota Corona out to the road and drove off, then she opened the door and walked in.

There were a large number of shoes lying inside the door where they had been removed by visitors, and the cold air in the hall still carried a hint of Ryuta's after-shave.

Toko walked through the house, stunned with disbelief; the light was on in the large living room, but she saw no signs of anyone there. She continued down the hall until she came to two Japanese-style rooms that faced the garden, and looking through a half-open door, she saw Ryuta's wife, Hisako, sitting there. She was two years younger than Ryuta and had always been a very reserved but kindly woman. It was probably because she did not have any children of her own, but like her husband she had always been very good to Toko and treated her more as a daughter than a niece.

Toko ran blindly to her side and hugged her tightly as she burst into tears. "What shall we do, Aunty. What shall we do? How could Uncle Ryuta . . . ?" She sobbed desperately until Hisako whispered soothingly in her ear.

"Don't worry, Toko, Uncle Ryuta is all right; he will be home soon. He would never do a silly thing like crash his airplane. He is indestructible, he will live forever. Just you wait and see, he will be home any minute now. . . ."

Toko looked up at Hisako's face in disbelief and realized that she was not crying at all, just gazing into space with a slight smile playing on her lips.

Hisako did not believe that her husband was dead. No, she probably realized, deep down that it was true, but her heart refused to accept it. By denying reality in that way, she was able to keep herself under control, at least temporarily.

"I always said that no good would come of his flying around in an airplane like that. They are not for amateurs, and it was only a question of time before he had an accident.''

The voice came from behind her, and Toko swung around in surprise to see a woman in her midforties with her hair dyed almost blond who was sitting facing Hisako. She had well-defined features and was very beautiful in a cold kind of way. She was wearing a very expensive-looking silver-gray kimono and looked as if she had hurried straight over upon hearing the news.

''He was always saying things like 'It could never happen to me,' or 'If an accident saw me coming, it would turn around and run away,' but life isn't as simple as that. It's frightening; he has had his own way for so long that he thought nothing could ever go wrong and so he went flying around in that damn plane of his. But something was bound to happen in the end.''

The woman had a very harsh voice and a most unusual intonation, which grated on the nerves of the listener. Although she very small in stature, she managed to be quite overpowering.

''It would be all right if it was a case of an accident just giving him a shock, but with a plane, that's not very likely. The head of a large company has no right to act in such a rash manner; if he had thought about his responsibility to the people he employs, he'd never have behaved so selfishly. Goodness knows how often I warned Ryuta about it. . . .''

She talked on and on without a pause until Toko felt that she wanted to shout at her to stop or to put her hands over her ears and cut off the sound of her voice.

Who *is* this woman? she thought. Who was she to warn Uncle Ryuta about anything?

It was then that she realized that it must be Yaeko Ichihara, the other person who shared the post of managing director with her father. Now that she came to think about it, Toko seemed to remember having seen her sitting with the other executives at Okito's funeral and recalled her mother once telling her about the woman.

''Yaeko used to run a bar in the Ginza area and was Okito's

lover. However, when he started to lose favor at the company, she switched to Ryuta, who gave her a position on the board of directors and then later made her a managing director."

Toko wished that Yaeko would just shut up; Hisako was having a hard enough time dealing with her loss without having her husband's lover antagonize her like this. But Yaeko seemed oblivious to Toko's glaring and continued to intrude on their grief.

"I suppose Ryuta was not really cut out to be the president of the company. I used to become so irritated at the way he carried on without a thought about anyone else. When I think about it, I realize that all the Shirafuji men must have a bit of insanity in them—Okito is an obvious case in point, although it was such a terrible waste. He was probably one of the greatest geniuses of the century and yet he died such an ignominious death. Ryuta said that he had brought it upon himself, but now Ryuta has . . ."

Toko sensed someone out in the hallway and felt a sense of relief flow through her. She looked up and saw the silhouette of a tall thin person walking toward them through the gloom. He had longish hair, a delicate nose, and his eyes glinted under thick eyebrows. His lips were well formed, his chin rather prominent, and there was something about him that gave him a vaguely Caucasian look.

For a moment she thought that it was Okito and that she had only dreamed his death, but that couldn't be. She stared at the man in amazement.

I have got to remain calm or I will go mad, too, she thought.

The man stopped at the entrance to the room and looked over at where Toko, Hisako, and Yaeko were sitting.

"Did you just say that Okito Shirafuji died an ignominious death?" he asked, his voice strangely quiet and his eyes fixed on Yaeko's face. It would appear that her harsh words had been quite audible down the hallway. "What do you think gives you the right to comment on someone else's death? You never know how you will die when your time comes."

Even Yaeko appeared to be at a loss for words and sat looking at him, her mouth dropping open in surprise.

"The only ones who know whether their death was suitable for them or not are the dead. At least I think that is true, for my father and I would not be surprised if he is standing on top of a cloud right now, laughing at the people he left behind."

As soon as he had mentioned his father, Toko's mind went back to that day, many years ago, when she had stood alone in the sand pit and watched as the long-legged boy walked away from her toward the house.

III

The funeral for Ryuta Shirafuji, president of Ruco Corporation, was held two days after the accident on Thursday, May 14, at one in the afternoon. The service was held at the Zenpukuji Temple, which was located near his house in Ogikubo.

The Five Lakes police station arranged for the body to be transported to his home at a little after nine o'clock on the evening of the twelfth, and the wake was held the following night. The private funeral was held on the fourteenth and the public memorial service was set for two weeks later at the Aoyana Cemetery.

The weather changed dramatically after the thirteenth; the clear blue sky was replaced by heavy clouds, there were strong gusts of wind, and occasionally heavy drops of rain dashed themselves against the windows.

If only the weather had changed a day earlier, Uncle Ryuta would never have gone flying. . . .

Toko knew that it would do no good thinking like this, but she could not help herself.

Although it was supposedly private, the funeral was attended by all the executives from Ruco and their customers, and no expense had been spared. The coffin was carried from the house at three o'clock and it was six o'clock before everyone left the crematorium and made their way back to the temple, Hisako clutching the urn containing the ashes to her breast.

When the group reached the temple, the whole family and the people from Ruco, about thirty people in all, sat down for a meal in one of the rooms at the back of the building. The family group consisted of Ryuta's widow, Hisako; his brother Koji, his wife, and the families of his two married daughters; Okito's son, Akihito; and Hiroshi, Sachiko, and Toko. Representing the company, were Yaeko Ichihara; her son, Hikaru, who also worked for the company, together with his wife; the staff who had been with the company from its very beginning, and the executives.

Depending on the age and position of the deceased, the meal after a funeral is sometimes a very subdued affair, but not in Ryuta's case. He was the founder of Ruco and it was due to his skill as a manager, his sense of the market, and his powerful personality that the company expanded as it had, until it reached its present preeminent position, at the top of its field and with employees numbering over three thousand. With his sudden disappearance, nobody could foresee the company's future, and everyone wondered who would be capable enough to take over his position as president. In terms of seniority, Koji was next in succession, but no one was sure if he had what it took to run the company.

Ryuta had been taken from them in his prime, and the people who had gathered together for his funeral all shared very mixed emotions over his death. They felt sorrow and a sense of loss, but at the same time they felt fear and uncertainty about the future. They sat white-faced and talked to each other in a rather desultory fashion.

Ryuta's death was all the harder to take coming as it did only fifty days after his brother's, who, it seemed, had not died of natural causes either. It was beginning to seem as if the Shirafuji family was cursed, and a little seed of fear gnawed at the hearts of each of the mourners.

Koji, who should have taken over from Ryuta as the head of the family, was still in a state of shock and had yet to do anything about the future. He was fifty-two years old, and although he bore a strong physical resemblance to Ryuta, he had grown up in the shadow of his elder brother and seemed nothing more than a smaller version of him. Having worked originally for a bank, he tended to involve himself with the financial side of the business and had been happy to leave the actual running of the company in Ryuta's capable hands. He did not have any clear idea of which way the company ought to proceed in the future and had always simply agreed with anything that Ryuta had suggested.

In order to hide his uncertainty about the future, Koji had immersed himself in the details of the accident and he used this as a method to forestall having to deal with any awkward questions.

"The first report came into the head office at 10:47 in the morning the day before yesterday. It was from Chofu Airfield, and I happened to be in the office just then, so I remember the time quite clearly. I hurried straight to the site of the accident. . . ." Before the meal started, he had felt that it was incumbent on him to make a speech of some kind, so he launched—not for the first time—into his account of the accident.

"About forty minutes after I arrived, the crash investigation team finally put in an appearance and started taking pictures and collecting the wreckage. They told me that they expected to be there for three days and would be making a full investigation of the circumstances leading to the accident. Since then, I have remained in touch with the local police at Five Lakes and they have kept me up to date on their progress."

"Have they learned anything new?" Hikaru Ichihara asked eagerly. He was still only twenty-four or -five, and due to his mother's influence, he was already assistant chief of the public relations department. He was wearing a fashionable pair of glasses under his broad, shiny forehead and he seemed to be a very shrewd young man.

"They haven't come to any definite decision yet, but it still seems likely that the accident was caused by water condensation in the fuel tank."

"Didn't Mr. Shirafuji say something about that when he was talking to the control tower by radio?" Hikaru asked.

"Yes, the control tower has a tape of the conversation."

"So," Hikaru concluded, "it was an unavoidable accident then."

"We cannot say that yet; we have to wait for the results of the investigation."

Of course everyone was very interested to discuss the cause of the accident, but if that was all Koji knew, they had heard it from him before. At the beginning, everyone listened to him out of politeness, but as the meal progressed they started to chat among themselves.

Toko sat alone on one side of the room near the corridor. Her father, Hiroshi, was talking with people from work and her mother was helping the girls from the office, who were in the kitchen making tea. Toko knew that she should really go out and offer to help, too, but she felt completely exhausted and could not bear the thought of having to talk to people.

It seemed as if years had passed since she talked to Ryuta on the telephone, and yet the conversation kept repeating itself in her head. She guessed that apart from the people in the control tower, she was probably the last person to have spoken to him. She remembered saying *I wish you wouldn't go up today,* and she regretted now that she hadn't been more insistent about stopping him. *Well, I must be going now; you never know, I might meet Okito on top of the clouds,* he had said as he hung up, and she wondered if something really had happened up there above the clouds. If it had not, it seemed impossible to her that Ryuta could have made a silly little mistake like not checking for condensation in the fuel tank; he was indestructible, he would not die. That was what Hisako had said two days earlier, and strangely, the idea had taken a hold in Toko's mind.

She looked over to see where Hisako was and noticed that she was sitting in the place of honor at the table. Her head was bowed and she made no effort to eat the foot that had been set before her; the only movement she made was to dab her handkerchief to her eyes every now and again. It was terrible to see her in such pain, but at least she had finally accepted the fact of her husband's death.

Two nights ago, Akihito's sudden appearance had served to put an end to Yaeko's spiteful comments. When he had said, *Who knows when or how you will die when your time comes?* even Yaeko seemed embarrassed and was quiet for a short while, but then she started asking him all sorts of personal questions.

"So you're Akihito, are you? Okito's son? I hear that when your father died, you were rushing around the world somewhere and nobody knew how to get in contact with you. You put Koji to a lot of trouble, you know. You didn't even come to the funeral. What on earth were you doing?"

Akihito had arrived back in Japan a few days after the funeral, and although Yaeko must have seen him at the memorial service, she spoke to him coldly, as if it were the first time they had met. "Okito led a lonely life toward the end, and I feel sure it would have been much easier for him if he could have had you at his side. What on earth were you doing abroad?" she repeated.

Akihito hardly said a word in reply to her callous comments; he just frowned irritably and soon walked back out down the dark hallway. Toko guessed that having rushed over to the house after hearing the news about Ryuta, he was unlikely to go home again immediately but would be walking around the house somewhere, reliving his memories of previous visits here when he was a boy. She felt a sudden urge to run after him, but forced herself to remain where she was.

Today, Toko had heard Yaeko's ceaseless chatter whenever she turned. After the wake the previous night, she had returned to her house, changed into a fresh mourning kimono, put a black pearl ring on her finger, and was back at the Shirafuji house by ten o'clock.

Toko had remained at the house since the day of the accident. Sachiko had shown up later with a change of clothing, and the two of them had stayed to help Hisako deal with guests, contact people to inform them of the wake, and do a thousand and one other things that could not be left in the hands of the undertakers. The body had been taken to the temple a little before noon and the service had started at one o'clock.

"What? This ring?" It was Yaeko's piercing voice again. "Yes, it was a present from Ryuta. It is rare to find a black pearl as perfect as this, and he told me that he came across it by accident at a jeweler's in Ginza and just couldn't resist buying it. He said he thought it would be perfect for me and I laughed, saying that he probably said that to all the girls, but I never dreamed that I'd be wearing it at his own funeral and so soon. . . ."

As she heard Yaeko's endless chatter, Toko looked up, and saw her sitting in the middle of the room, surrounded by the other relatives and making herself the center of attention.

"Maybe Okito didn't like it by himself and called his brother to keep him company," Yaeko said. "He always was a very lonely individual. . . ."

"Yes, they were always very close," one of the relatives said.

"Yes," Yaeko said. "I have never seen brothers who cared for each other so much. I suppose that due to their difference in age, Ryuta always felt very protective toward him. It's a shame, really, that Okito was such a genius, that's the only thing that stood between them. . . ."

Toko feared that Yaeko might say something to irritate Akihito again. Her eyes went to the head table, but he was not there. He had sat quietly with the rest of the family during the service, but although he had come to the room after the body was cremated, he had disappeared again afterward. He obviously did not like sitting with the rest of the family, and Toko realized that he must find it very difficult to fit in. She was glad, however, that he had not heard the way that Yaeko was talking.

Toko had felt devoid of emotion since she had first heard

of the accident and yet, strangely, she felt her heart go out to Akihito.

"Things were much better in the old days, weren't they?" Yaeko was saying now. "I remember—oh, it must have been soon after the company was first started as I still had my business in Ginza; sometime around '67 or '8, Ryuta brought Okito around to my shop—"

Her voice suddenly stopped in midsentence. She was sitting on the same side of the table as Toko and there were several people between them, so Toko could not see her, but she could hear her panting for breath for a few moments.

"Ryuta must have been about thirty-five or -six and Okito was still in his twenties, but I remember Ryuta saying, 'My brother here is going to make great inventions one day, just you wait and see. The future of Ruco rests on his skill at inventing and my . . . my entrepreneurial . . .' Please excuse me a moment. . . ."

She stood up and, passing behind Toko, made her way out to the corridor. She was a small woman, but she had a good figure, and she looked very beautiful, even in her mourning clothes. She held her hands out slightly as if she were unsure of her balance and the black pearl on her finger flashed brightly.

Without thinking, Toko stood up and followed her. The other guests, simply assuming that Yaeko was going to the bathroom, did not give her a second thought, but Toko sensed, somehow, that something was wrong. And besides, she felt that she could not bear to remain in the room a moment longer.

Yaeko pushed open the door at the end of the corridor to reveal another large room with a corridor to one side. Nobody was using the room at this time and it was quite dark, except for a small night-light. Yaeko entered and closed the door behind her, but Toko soon opened it again and followed her down the corridor.

The sun had set a short while before and the stone lanterns in the garden had been lit to reveal some pretty purple flowers growing there.

Yaeko walked around the corner at the end of the corridor,

and by now she was starting to stagger slightly. The corridor continued around the corner and this time it faced onto a small enclosed courtyard. Halfway down, a man in mourning dress was standing alone, looking out at the night, and when Toko saw his profile, she realized that it was Akihito. He was frowning slightly as he stared into the garden and she guessed that he was probably thinking about his father or his uncle's death. He was so absorbed that he did not seem to notice the sound of the two women approaching.

By this time, Yaeko was definitely unsteady on her feet. Toko seemed to remember that there was a bathroom at the end of this corridor, and she guessed that when Yaeko first started to feel unwell, she had decided to go and sit down there alone, where she would not be seen.

Yaeko was just two or three steps away from Akihito when he realized she was there and swung around toward her in surprise. At that moment, she staggered and fell forward, reaching out instinctively for him. He reached out and managed to catch her arms, but he was unable to support her; her knees hit the floor and she collapsed, facedown, on the floor.

"Yaeko!" both Toko and Akihito cried, then rushed to her and knelt down on either side of the slight figure that lay crumpled on the wooden floor. Her face was flushed a strange dark red.

Akihito shook her shoulders and then put his hand to her forehead.

"She has a terrible fever!" he exclaimed.

"So she does," agreed Toko. She had taken one of her hands, but was shocked by the unnatural warmth of it. "We must call a doctor," she said, then gave a gasp. "Look, blood."

She was holding Yaeko's right hand, but there was a small flow of blood coming from the other one, near the base of the finger that was wearing the pearl ring.

"She has injured herself."

"But how could she hurt herself in a place like that?"

The pearl on the bloodstained finger was more than half an inch in diameter and shone with a sinister light.

3

The Mystery of the
Black Pearl

It was two o'clock on the afternoon of May 16 at the Ogikubo police station on the Ome Road. The station chief, his assistant, the chief of the detective section, and the chief of the homicide team were all together in the chief's office. The rain that had been falling since the thirteenth had finally stopped and it was a beautiful spring day.

"Forensics got in touch with us around noon today with the results of the autopsy on Yaeko Ichihara and that's why I asked you all to step in here," Assistant Inspector Wakao of the homicide team said, looking down at his notebook. "Just to fill in those of you who are new to the case, Ms. Ichihara was forty-five years old and an executive at the Ruco Corporation. Two days ago, she went to the Zenpukuji Temple to attend the funeral of the company president, Ryuta Shirafuji, who died recently in an aircraft accident, but during the meal after the service, she suddenly left the room and walked along the corridor in the direction of the bathroom. She never made it that far, however, and at about 6:20, she collapsed in front of two members of the Shirafuji family.''

She had an extremely high temperature and was barely conscious, so she was rushed by ambulance to the nearby Igusa hospital. She remained in that condition for one day until she died at approximately 5:00 P.M. on May 15. She never regained consciousness.

"The doctor in charge said that her condition was very similar to septicemia,'' the assistant inspector continued, "but there were several things that did not seem to fit. In particular, there was a scratch on her ring finger just above the bottom joint that was bleeding when she was brought in. The two people who discovered her and the crew of the ambulance also remarked on this, which would mean that she had received the scratch before she lost consciousness.''

When the other men looked up at him inquiringly, he produced a ring from an envelope and placed it on the table in front of them.

"The deceased was wearing this ring on the finger in question and the scratch was formed just behind it. The people at the hospital noticed that a small barb had been lifted up in the platinum mount where it touches the finger, and this would probably be sufficient to cause the scratch after a period of time. This was not all they found, though.''

The other three men all leaned forward to get a better look at the ring while Wakao explained.

"A ring of this kind generally has a small open space in the mount behind the stone, and this one is no exception, except that in this case, it would appear to have been filled with some kind of ointment, and there are also indications that this was sealed in with wax. It's possible that if the ring was worn, the wax could melt, allowing the ointment to enter the body through the wound that was caused by the barb in the platinum. For this reason, the hospital considered the possibility of foul play in causing Ms. Ichihara's death and contacted us.''

The previous night, Inspector Wakao had telephoned the station chief at home and, after telling him about the hospital's suspicions, had arranged for the body to be sent to the police hospital for an autopsy together with the ring; naturally he had received the deceased's relatives' permission before doing so.

The autopsy had taken place that morning and Wakao had gone to the police hospital in Otsuka to hear the results directly from the doctor who had performed it.

"What was the result?" he asked, pausing dramatically.

Wakao looked very serious and, picking up a piece of paper from the table in front of him, started to read from it.

"Traces of lysin were found in the wound on the ring finger of the deceased. The space in the rear of the ring was found to contain a small amount of a paste, which contained a large quantity of lysin. The symptoms displayed by the deceased were consistent with those produced by lysin poisoning, and so it is considered highly likely that Yaeko Ichihara died of a fatal dose of lysin."

"Lysin?" asked the assistant chief. It was obvious from his expression that he had never heard the name before.

"Yes, this is the conclusion the doctor came to after discussing it with one of his colleagues who majored in biochemistry at the same university the doctor had attended. Apparently it is a poisonous protein that is found in the seeds of the castor-oil plant, and it is considered to be one of the five most poisonous substances in the world. The minutest quantity is sufficient to cause death, and lysin is unusual in that it takes at least ten hours from the time it is administered before it has any visible effect on the victim. Symptoms of lysin poisoning are shivering, high fever, and delirium, and it can easily be mistaken for blood poisoning."

"How much is necessary for a fatal dose?"

"Er . . . point zero three milligrams per kilogram of body weight. That means that for someone weighing one hundred and ten pounds, one point five milligrams or about the size of a match head would be adequate."

"Do we know how much Yaeko Ichihara weighed?" Inspector Dan, the chief of the detective section broke in.

"Yes, she was weighed before the autopsy," Wakao replied. "She was very slightly built and only weighed eighty-seven-point-five pounds, so if we call that ninety pounds, only about point-zero-four of an ounce would be necessary to cause death. The amount varies from person to person, however, and upon their condition at the time of ingestion, so it's likely that for a woman who was exhausted from the shock of Ryuta Shirafuji's death and lack of sleep, not even that much would have been sufficient."

"Anyway, if it would only take an amount about the size of a match head, it is quite possible that the lysin hidden in her ring could have done the trick," the station chief said. He picked up the ring for the first time and studied it carefully. The pearl was so large that there was a space in the back about one-third of an inch square by one-fifth of an inch high. Here and there, traces of wax and dried ointment could be seen sticking to the edges, and near the spot where this would come in contact with the skin, the platinum had been cut to form a sharp barb. He slipped it onto his little finger, but it would only go halfway down. He grimaced slightly, and when he took the ring off, they could see a small scratch on the middle of his thick finger. It was not deep enough to draw blood, but it was quite clear.

"I see," the station chief said, nodding, "if you were to wear this for any length of time, it would keep scratching your finger until eventually it drew blood."

"Yes," Inspector Dan agreed, "although it would be a little painful, it wouldn't be unbearable and Yaeko had probably put up with it until the lysin entered her bloodstream, and then it was too late."

"I can see that we're going to have to question her acquaintances a bit more closely to find out what happened, but in the meantime, I would like to suggest my own theory," Wakao said.

"Yaeko had been wearing her ring ever since she left her house on the morning of the fourteenth, and as the chief just said, although it was a little painful, it was not unbearable. However, at about 6:20 or thereabouts, she had for some reason pressed it directly above the barb and this had been sufficient to cause it to draw blood." Wakao continued. "Usually, she would have taken it off at this point, but at the same time, she suddenly felt sick or something and stood up to go to the bathroom. She had probably felt unwell for some time, but had forced herself to ignore it until the funeral was over. However, at the time in question, she couldn't stand it any longer and walked out to the corridor, where she collapsed. Or at least, that's how I see the course of events."

"The first thing we must check on, though," Inspector Dan said, clearly dubious, "is whether it would really have been possible for the lysin in the ring to enter the body in sufficient quantity to cause death."

Wakao responded quickly. "Apparently, this cannot be ruled out and there is no denying the fact that she died of lysin poisoning. While it is possible that she could have been administered a fatal dose orally, it's just as feasible for the poison to have entered through the wound on her finger. Both the doctor who did the autopsy and the professor in biochemistry agree on this point."

"That may be true," Dan responded, "but it seems a bit farfetched somehow."

"It's not as rare as you may think. I heard from forensics that lysin has been used in some very well-known murders." Wakao looked down at his papers again. "Not all that long ago, in 1978, a Bulgarian writer who had defected to Britain was walking along the embankment next to the river Thames when someone suddenly stabbed him in the thigh with an umbrella. It didn't hurt too much at the time and he didn't worry about it, but at about two o'clock the following morning he developed a high fever and became delirious. He was admitted to a hospital but died two days later. Scotland Yard performed an autopsy and found a small metal sphere, about one-sixteenth of an inch across, embedded in his thigh. There was a small hole in the sphere that showed signs of having been sealed with wax, and it was guessed that this had melted to release the contents of the sphere into the bloodstream. They soon managed to analyze the contents as having been lysin.

"A short while later, another defector in Paris was stabbed in the back with an umbrella and it was discovered that he also had a small metal capsule in the wound, exactly the same as the London one. After this, lysin become the poison of choice for spies in fiction and it is probable that the murderer read about it somewhere."

This was the first time the word "murderer" had been used.

"All the same . . ." Inspector Dan shook his head. He was thirty-nine years old and quite young for his rank. He looked like a sophisticated city person, but he spoke with a broad country accent from the north of Japan that gave away his roots. "I might understand it if Yaeko Ichihara had been a spy or something, but why should the murderer use such a roundabout method to murder her? Why didn't he just slip some rat poison into her food or something?"

Wakao, who was still only thirty-two and quite plump and rather bearlike in appearance, looked back at his superior defiantly. "Perhaps he was not able to do it by any other method."

"Why not? Can you be a little more precise?"

"Well, er . . ." Wakao could not come up with a reason right away and bit his lip in frustration.

II

"Lysin is one of the five most poisonous substances known to man and is quite deadly. It is produced from the seeds of the castor-oil plant, and as the oil is used for everything from machines to paints, it is quite common in factories and laboratories throughout the country.

"This kind of natural poison is much stronger than its man-made counterparts. For instance, cyanide is probably the best known of the man-made poisons, but the poison to be found in the common blowfish is thirty thousand times as strong, and botulism is an unbelievable one billion times as deadly. This means that when using natural poisons, only the minutest amounts are necessary.''

Wakao watched the expressions of disgust and interest that appeared on the faces of the five people sitting in front of him as he expounded on his newly attained knowledge.

It was Sunday, May 17, and Yaeko Ichihara's house was filled with an unusual number of people and a terrible atmosphere of gloom. It was a small, wooden, two-story house built in traditional Japanese style. There was a black and white vertical striped curtain hung on the fence outside to signify that it was in mourning and every room was filled with the smell of incense.

The Ruco Corporation had lost yet another executive in extremely strange circumstances, and although Yaeko was not an actual member of the Shirafuji clan, it was an open secret that she had been involved with Okito and later Ryuta. She had always behaved as if she was one of the family, and when she died, people all thought as if the family had lost another member.

This time suspicious circumstances were undeniably involved in the death, and to make things worse, the victim had collapsed at Ryuta's funeral and never regained consciousness again. Rumors were surfacing that the Ruco Corporation was cursed, and feeling very conscious of this, the company made every effort to keep Yaeko's funeral as quiet as possible.

The wake was held on the sixteenth, after the body was returned from the autopsy, and the funeral was held the next day. Despite the fact that the company wanted to keep everything low-key, they could do nothing to stop the police from arriving at the service and starting to make inquiries around the neighborhood.

By the morning of the seventeenth, all the evidence seemed to point toward the fact that Yaeko had been murdered—it being unlikely that anyone would choose such a complicated way to commit suicide—and so a murder headquarters was set up at Ogikubo police station.

Wakao was so eager to get down to work that he arrived at Yaeko's house at one o'clock, an hour before the service was due to begin. He found most of the relatives already gathered there, and ignoring their suspicious looks, he asked Koji to arrange for everyone who had been seated near Yaeko at Ryuta's funeral to step into another room.

None of them were eager to talk to him, but they obviously thought it best to cooperate with the police, and soon five of the Shirafuji family were gathered in a small room next to the main entrance.

In order to make sure they all knew why they had been called out, Wakao explained what he knew of the circumstances behind Yaeko's death and then gave them a short lecture on lysin.

"So you see that while natural poisons like this are much stronger than man-made ones, it is difficult to produce them in any quantity, and that is why they are not so readily available. Lysin is commonly used by spies for their executions; this is probably because they need only use the minutest amounts to kill their victims."

He thought of telling them about the umbrella murders in London and Paris nine years earlier, but decided this would not be necessary and dropped into silence for a moment. He licked his lips before continuing.

"Of course, this is not to say that we think that Ms. Ichihara was a spy or anything, although we will look into it just to be sure. What we want to hear about from you is the way she behaved immediately before her death. Lysin takes a long time to have any physical effect and we want to know if she said anything that might indicate any awareness on her part of what was happening to her or who might have wanted to kill her."

Nobody spoke.

"I have been told that you were the people who were sitting closest to her after you all returned to the temple from the crematorium." He looked over at Koji's wife Harue, his daughter Kaori, and Yaeko's daughter-in-law Fujiko as he spoke.

Everyone had felt very relieved after the cremation and had relaxed for the meal at the temple, sitting more or less where they wanted. Yaeko had made use of her position as Ryuta's mistress to leave the bar she had run in Ginza and get a job at Ruco, eventually rising to the post of managing director. Rumor had it, though, that recently Yaeko was moving in on Koji, and this could be seen by the way she had managed to seat herself in between his wife and daughter. The three women looked uncomfortable under his scrutiny.

"When did she start to behave strangely?" Wakao asked.

They all exchanged looks, then Harue took it upon herself to act as spokeswoman.

"Yes, well, I'm afraid that we didn't notice anything really. Yaeko was as bright as ever, chatting away and making herself the center of attention as usual. When I thought about it later, though, she did seem to look a bit tired and sometimes she sort of panted for breath a little. . . ."

"Yes, and she did not have very much appetite. Father always used to laugh about the amount she managed to eat considering how small she was," Kaori added. She was twenty-seven years old and was already married. "However, she hardly lifted her chopsticks at all during the meal and I remember thinking it a bit strange."

"Did she seem to be pained by the finger with the ring on it?"

"Oh, yes, I suppose she was."

They all nodded in agreement.

"She kept twisting the ring with her other hand, but then she always behaved like that when she was wearing a ring that she was especially fond of."

"She was very proud of that black pearl of hers, she had been fiddling with it ever since she first put it on this morning."

"I see, so you are saying that it was a habit of hers and therefore you didn't pay it any particular attention. Now, if we can go back over the events of the fourteenth. She returned home after the wake, changed, put on the black pearl ring, and returned to the Shirafuji house in Ogikubo, is that right? What time would you say it was that she put the ring on and left this house?'' Wakao addressed his questions to Fujiko, who had not spoken much. She looked about twenty-four or -five and appeared to be a little older than her husband Hikaru.

"I don't know," she replied brusquely. "My husband and I live in an apartment in Yakumo, not here with her."

"Oh yes, I had forgotten. Did your mother-in-law live here on her own?"

"Yes, but she did have a maid who came in five days a week to clean for her."

"Is she here today?"

"Of course, I saw her in the kitchen just now."

Wakao made a mental note to interview the maid later, but he realized that as Yaeko had lived on her own, it was going to be very difficult for him to find out any details of her life. It occurred to him that there had been another, similar case recently where very little had been discovered about the victim and then he remembered that this victim had been Okito Shirafuji. For the first time his confidence in their ability to solve the case started to waver.

"To get back to the ring again, did any of you notice that the finger she was wearing it on was bleeding slightly?"

"Er . . . ," stammered Kaori.

"She did mention the ring," Harue said, "but only to say that Ryuta had bought it for her. She sounded very emotional about it."

"I think that if it had been bleeding, we would have noticed it," Kaori said.

Wakao left them for a moment and turned toward the couple who were sitting to one side.

"It is Toko Chino and Akihito Shirafuji, isn't it? I believe you two just happened to be in the corridor near Yaeko when she collapsed, is that correct? Did you have any reason for stepping out into the corridor when you did, Ms. Chino?"

"No, I didn't, it was just that . . ." Toko was at a loss as to what to say, then she decided to just tell him everything as it happened.

"Yaeko suddenly stood up, and when I saw her leave the room, I felt that there was something odd about her behavior."

"Was she unsteady on her feet or something?"

"Yes, I suppose so, that must have been it."

"Did you notice that her finger was bleeding?"

"Not until she collapsed in the corridor. She had flung her left hand out and we noticed that there was blood coming from under her ring."

Wakao looked over at Akihito.

"That's right," Akihito agreed in a deep, slightly sullen voice. He realized that Wakao was going to ask what he was doing in the corridor on his own, so he added, "I wanted to have a smoke without worrying about the other people, so I left the room for a while."

"Could you give me a detailed description of what happened when she collapsed?"

"Yes, I didn't look around and see her until she was almost upon me . . . ." He went on to explain how Yaeko had reached out to him for support, but although he had caught her hands, he had not been able to stop her falling to the floor. "I realized right away that she had an unnaturally high temperature."

"Did you notice that her finger was bleeding?"

"Toko noticed it first and pointed it out to me." He turned his dark, deep-set eyes on Toko, who nodded in agreement.

"I see, so I suppose we must assume that the wound on her finger became worse as she was walking along the corridor and finally started to bleed. You two would appear to be the first to notice that she was not feeling well—if you should remember anything else, please get in touch with me at the investigation headquarters at the Ogikubo station."

Akihito nodded, then turned his gaze on Toko again, and she felt an inexplicable thrill rush through her body. She guessed that it must be because they had both been present when Yaeko collapsed and the experience had brought them together. It was strange, but despite the terrible things that had happened, first to Okito, then to Ryuta, and finally to Yaeko, her heart seemed to beat with a different rhythm ever since they had met. On the day of Ryuta's accident, when she had gone to comfort Hisako, she had seen his tall silhouette in the corridor, and her first thought had been that it was Okito. Oddly, since that day, she seemed to have risen earlier each morning. At that moment, something seemed to have changed in her, but she still could not understand what it was.

III

Yaeko's body was cremated and her ashes brought back to her house. Soon it was time for the first seven-day memorial and a meal was prepared and guests invited. Although such an event was no more than customary, nobody could forget the fact that it had been at just such a meal as this, after Ryuta's funeral, that Yaeko had collapsed. A number of the guests could not get over the feeling that a similar thing would happen again and were terrified.

The directors of Ruco and relatives just wanted to finish the funeral with as little fuss as possible, and if any of the guests indicated that they wanted to return home without stopping for the meal, they did not make much effort to stop them.

Toko's father, Hiroshi, as one of the executives of the company, had to stay, but her mother, Sachiko, took Toko aside and whispered, "If you want to get on back to the house, nobody'd mind."

"What about you?"

"They need me to help out in the kitchen, so I'll stay a little longer."

"Really? Well, if you're sure you don't mind . . ."

"Make sure you have something to eat when you get back."

"Okay."

Sachiko thought Toko had lost weight since Ryuta's death and she was worried about her daughter's health.

After leaving the house, Toko walked down the hill through the quiet residential neighborhood toward the station. Dusk had already fallen, and looking up, she saw the stars already filling the sky. In Japan, it is said that when you die, you become a star, and she wondered if Okito and Ryuta were among the countless stars looking down on her. Left on her own, she soon felt very lonely and sad, and her thoughts went out to Akira Takubo. She had not seen him since the day of Ryuta's crash, but he had telephoned her every other day to make sure she was okay. She saw a telephone booth nearby and decided to call him.

Akira had originally come from Tsuru City in Yamanashi prefecture, but now he was living in a small apartment near the university in the Chiyoda area. It was a little before seven and she guessed that he would probably be home now. He had often told her that his mother insisted on sending him packages of food all the time, and as he did not like to let it go to waste, he ate at home as much as possible.

She dialed his number from memory and soon heard it ring. Once . . . twice . . . three times . . . He picked it up on the fourth ring.

At that moment, a black Porsche Carrera pulled up outside the phone booth and the driver nodded toward her. She looked closer, and in the light of the booth, she could make out a man's thin, well-formed features.

She gasped. "Uncle Okito . . ."

"Hello?" came a voice.

"Hello?" it repeated irritably; it was Akira's.

The driver of the car sat looking forward, leaving the car where it was. It was a sleek, classic sports car with low windows, and she could see his fingers beating a tattoo against the door.

I'm sorry, Akira, but something important has come up, she said silently.

She hung up the phone and pushed open the door of the booth.

Akihito looked out of the window and said, "I saw your

silhouette through the window of the booth and wondered if I could give you a lift to the station.''

"Oh, thank you, it's very kind."

He opened the passenger door and she hurried around the car to slip in next to him. She felt as if she had half expected him to turn up all along.

There was music playing quietly on the stereo.

"Where abouts do you live?" he asked as the car pulled away from the curb.

"In Naka-Meguro. In between Meguro-dori Avenue and Komazawa-dori Avenue."

"It'll be quickest to go down Meguro-dori Avenue then, won't it?" he said, and flicked his right-turn signal.

"You know your way well."

"Hmm?"

"I mean considering the amount of time you have been living abroad, you know your way around Tokyo well."

"Yes, but I lived here until I graduated junior high and I still remember it quite well. Anyway, it's been a month and a half since my father died and I've been moving around the city every day since then."

"Is this your car?"

"Not a chance, it belongs to the company. Uncle Koji said I would need a car while I was in town and lent me this one. It's his kind of car and I imagine he had the company buy it for his own use."

Ryuta and Koji had been quite embarrassed by Okito's solitary death and Koji seemed to have decided to do all he could to look after Okito's only son, Akihito.

It being a Sunday, there were none of the usual rush-hour jams, but there were still a lot of cars on the road, and it was only Akihito's skill at driving that allowed them to get back as quickly as they did.

"That's it, can you turn left at that corner, please?"

"Will you be having dinner on your own when you get in?"

"Yes, I suppose so."

"Then why don't we go somewhere together for a meal. I haven't had anything yet, either."

The car was past the corner before she even answered.

"Are you staying at your father's house in Egota while you're in Tokyo?"

"Yes, although I sometimes stay in a hotel. My father lived on his own in that house for a long time, and it's a real mess. Not only that, but it's a Japanese-style house and I'm not used to sitting on the floor anymore. I'm doing my best, though, as I have to go through all my father's things—not that I've gotten very far yet."

"It must be a terrible job. I remember that it seemed as if every room was piled high with books and research papers."

"By the way, what would you like for dinner?"

"Anything, I'm not fussy."

"It's not far from here to the Shiroganedai Hotel; shall we go there?"

"Okay."

The car passed Meguro Station and soon pulled into the forecourt of the hotel.

"Are you staying here?"

"No, but I suppose I might stay here tonight," Akihito replied, and stepped out of the car. He led the way down to the basement of the hotel. "What would you say to some Italian food?"

"It sounds lovely."

He turned into a dark entrance opposite the main restaurant. Inside, it was much bigger than Toko had expected and the walls and ceilings were covered in colorful frescoes. There was a stage in front of the far wall where a foreigner was playing the guitar and singing. She also noticed a large number of foreigners among the diners. The waiter led them to a table with a pretty little red lamp on it.

"Do you drink, Toko?"

"Yes, I drink a little beer or wine now and again."

"Okay, I'll order half a bottle of the house wine, shall I? Is there anything that you particularly like or shall I just order a few things and we can share?"

Toko knew very little about Italian food and so she was grateful that he was there to choose for her and explain what everything was. They started with prosciutto and figs followed by two types of spaghetti, one with a tomato sauce and the other with a Bolognese sauce. For the main course, he chose cutlets, Milanese style, and grilled fish. The waiter appeared with a bottle of chilled wine.

"Cheers," Akihito said, and raised his glass to her. She raised her own glass and they touched with a faint ring.

"I feel exhausted. Funerals are terribly demanding, whether they're in the family or not." She could feel the warmth of the wine spread through her body.

"I didn't really need to attend the funeral myself," Akihito said, "but I happened to have been there when she collapsed, and I felt somehow obliged to see it through to the end."

"I suppose the same could be said for me. But it is a coincidence, isn't it, after what you said to her on the day of Uncle Ryuta's crash."

"What?"

"Don't you remember, you said, 'Who knows when or how you will die.' "

"Yes, now you mention it, I do seem to remember saying something like that." Akihito really seemed to have forgotten.

"And only two days later, it came true. I think that if nothing else, that was reason enough for you to come to the funeral today."

"You make it sound as if she died as a result of what I said. You don't mince your words, do you?"

Their hors d'oeuvres arrived, and as they picked up their forks, Toko asked, "What did you do for a living abroad?"

"Pottery."

"You mean that you're a potter?"

"Nothing very grand, but I have a small kiln in the suburbs of Paris where I fire semi-Oriental-style pots."

"Oh, I went to Paris once with Uncle Ryuta and we visited the potteries at Sèvres. Are you anywhere near there?"

"No, I am further south in the heart of the country. A place called Melun."

"How long have you been living there?"

"Only about three years. I graduated from Columbia University in 1981 and worked for an electronics company in New York for a couple of years—" He suddenly broke off and looked embarrassed. It would appear that he did not like to talk about himself.

"What did you do after that?" Toko urged, looking at him with interest.

After a short pause, he finally started to talk again. "While I was working in Manhattan, I got to know some of the artists who gather there . . . there are hundreds of them of all nationalities and I became very interested in pottery."

"I see."

"I was tired of office work, I had had enough of logic and calculations, I wanted to live a simpler life and make something with my own hands."

"I know just how you feel."

"I knew that I'd never be able to compare with my father when it came to working in electronics and so I made up my mind to get out of it. I handed in my notice and went to England."

"Didn't your father try to talk you out of it?"

"He didn't know. I didn't write to him about it until I had arrived in England. I presented him with a fait accompli, and anyway, this was in 1983, he was totally involved with his work and didn't have time to think about anything else."

After studying pottery in Cornwall for two years, Akihito had gone to France and decided to settle down in the suburbs of Paris. It had been three years now since he first opened his kiln and he was finally managing to make a living out of it, his works being displayed in a famous gallery in Paris.

That means he must be about twenty-eight now, Toko thought after a quick bit of calculation.

Their pasta dishes arrived and they shared half of each. It was difficult for Toko to believe that this was the first time they had ever had dinner together; their mood was so relaxed that she felt as if they ate like this every day.

"Did Uncle Okito ever visit your kiln?"

"No, never. I would send him a Christmas card every year and every now and again we would talk on the phone, but we were not really very close."

"So you did not know how he was . . ."

She was about to ask if he knew that his father had been addicted to alcohol and drugs for the last two or three years of his life, but she realized that it was not her place to tell him.

"No, men are not very good at talking to each other, even when they're father and son." He seemed to know what she had almost blurted and answered her with an expression of resigned sadness. "We never talked about our problems and always put on a bold front. Whenever we spoke on the phone, he would tell me that his research was going well and that it was only a question of time before he succeeded. I will admit that I wasn't always convinced, but I thought he was just going through a temporary problem and would solve it eventually. I thought that it best if I didn't come and see him while he was having difficulty, though, that I would wait a little longer until he had something to celebrate. At least that's what I told myself.

"It was my own fault, I should have guessed there was something wrong, but I wish that someone had contacted me and asked for my help. I know that I was away on vacation when he died and that nobody was able to find me, but normally, they only had to ask my father to find out my address and telephone number. No, I suppose I'm being selfish again; if I hadn't spent the last ten years enjoying myself abroad, it might never have come to this."

He shook his hair out of his eyes and, picking up his glass, emptied it in one gulp.

"All I can do now," he said in a subdued voice, "is talk to the people who knew him and try to learn as much as I can about the way he really was. That's the only way I'll ever get to know what kind of man he was."

He sat there in front of her, all his defenses down, and Toko felt her heart go out to him. Her thoughts went back to Okito with his boyish enthusiasm and Ryuta with his ambition—she could almost see them standing there in front of her—and she could hold back her tears no longer. She took her handkerchief out of her bag and wiped her eyes, then looked up to see that Akihito was still sitting with his eyes fixed on the table in front of him.

"Why is it, Toko, that nobody wants to talk to me about my father?" he asked in a subdued voice. "Ryuta, Koji, even your father all become very uneasy when I start to talk about him, and they try to change the subject as soon as they can."

"I think it must be very hard for them. They all feel a certain degree of guilt about the way Okito died, but to admit that would be to put the blame on Uncle Ryuta as it was his policy that led to Okito's death."

"Yes, I'm beginning to realize that now." Akihito looked up with a smile. "In fact that's one of the reasons why I invited you out this evening—I hoped that you might speak frankly to me about my father. Preferably, I'd like you to tell me about the happy times; I'd like to have some memories of him when he was smiling."

"That'll be easy," Toko said, half laughing, half crying. "Uncle Okito always seemed to go out of his way to be nice to me."

"Yes, I can understand why he would."

"You went to America when I was still seven or eight years old, and after that, Uncle Okito would often take me to the funfair or to a famous ice cream parlor. However, I have one very special memory of him."

She had relived this memory of him many times since he died and now it had become her most cherished remembrance of him. Although she had not realized it at the time, she had witnessed a very precious moment in Okito's life and she would never forget it.

"It was when I was fifteen, I was walking along the main street in the Ginza district when I ran into Okito. It was in the evening, I had been to an art gallery with some friends and was on my way back to Shinbashi Station on my own. . . ."

If Toko was fifteen, it must have been 1981. Okito was forty-two and had already realized that his research was not going as smoothly as he had hoped. The strain of failure was beginning to show on his face, but that day he had been wearing a smart suit and was with a beautiful woman in her midthirties.

When they met, Toko had meant to continue home on her own, but Okito had persuaded her to go with them to a restaurant somewhere. Okito had gradually become drunk, and finally, he had taken the woman's hand and looked over at Toko.

"This person is going to go far away from me, Toko," he said in a serious tone, "but our hearts will remain bound together forever."

The woman had a plump, gentle face and was wearing dark-colored clothes. She sat listening to Okito in silence, but finally tears began to well in the corners of her eyes and run down her pale cheeks.

This was the first time outside of the movies that Toko had ever seen a grown woman cry.

IV

The atmosphere in the room at the Ogikubo police station was tense that Sunday as the detectives connected with the case gathered to discuss their progress.

"I will start with a report on the origins of the lysin that was used to kill Yaeko Ichihara, shall I?" assistant Inspector Yuhara of headquarters asked by way of opening the proceedings. "My report is based mainly on what I was able to learn from the doctor who performed the autopsy and his colleague, the professor of biochemistry.

"As you already know, lysin is made from the seeds of the castor-oil plant. When I asked where these could be obtained, I was informed that it would be quite a simple matter. First, there are the laboratories in the medical, agricultural, pharmaceutical, and biochemical departments of all the main universities, and second, there are the factories and research laboratories of companies that use castor oil in their products. I'm afraid that we'll have to check each of these facilities, one by one, to see how the substances are kept, whether any of the employees have criminal records, and if any lysin has been missing recently."

The thirty-odd detectives who were gathered in the room nodded in agreement. They were glad that they finally had a clear goal in their investigations and were eager to get on with it.

"It's not going to be very easy, I'm afraid," Yuhara said, dampening the optimistic mood in the room. "I'm sure that when you heard the name 'lysin,' you all assumed that the investigation would be confined to pharmaceutical companies, but I'm afraid that it has countless other uses: lubrication, hair cream, electrical insulation, artificial leather, typewriter oil, brake oil, carbon paper, shoe polish, paint, and a thousand other things. Obviously, as it is so common, the number of factories using it is very large.

"On top of that, for someone with a basic knowledge of chemistry, extracting lysin from castor-oil seeds is rather easy. As they are in such common demand, the seeds are grown all over the country, and an even larger amount is imported every year. If someone could get hold of a mere handful of seeds, they could produce their own lysin without too much trouble."

"I see, and if the factories buy the seeds in bulk, they won't keep a very strict guard over them," the station chief added.

"It's not only the seeds; I doubt if they take very much trouble to look after the extracted lysin either. Everyone knows how lax they are at plating works about the way they store their cyanide; I think if lysin is used a lot in laboratories, they're not going to be very strict about its storage either. Finally, lysin is kept in powder form and it only takes the minutest quantity for a fatal dose, so even if someone were to steal some, there would be no way of telling afterward.''

A sigh went up around the room. It looked as if it were not going to be so easy to find where the poison came from after all. However, they had no choice at the moment but to check all the possible places the murderer could have obtained it. So saying, Inspector Yuhara resumed his seat.

''Next, I think we should hear the report on the pearl ring that was used,'' the station chief said, nodding toward Inspector Dan.

After a momentary hesitation, Inspector Dan began, ''The victim herself said that she was given the ring by Ryuta Shirafuji, who died two days before her, in an aircraft accident.'' Dan was over six feet tall and looked like the star of an action movie, but the image was spoiled the moment he opened his mouth since he spoke with a country accent from the northern part of Japan. ''Her son, Hikaru, and his wife, her housekeeper, and several of her colleagues at the company all swear to this, and on the day that she died, she had been telling the same thing to everyone who wanted to listen, so I think we can safely assume it was the truth.

''As to when she received it, she appeared wearing it at the company's foundation day party seven months ago, in October, and told several of the people it was a gift from the company's president. She said that he had come across it at a jeweler's in Ginza and had been so impressed by it that he had bought it on the spot. I therefore started by checking all the jeweler's in the Ginza area to see if they had sold a similar ring between September and October of last year.''

He spoke very slowly and several of the other detectives nodded impatiently in an effort to urge him on.

''Luckily, I came across a shop in the main street called Southern Cross, where the manager remembered both the ring and Mr. Shirafuji's purchase of it. I had him look up the date in his records; it was the twenty-sixth of September. Apparently he had arranged to meet a young lady outside the shop. She looked like a bar hostess or something, and as soon as she arrived, they both entered the shop, where he bought her a ruby ring. That was when he had first noticed the black pearl; he seemed to take an instant liking to it and bought it on the spot. He paid for both rings with a personal check and put the pearl ring in his own pocket.''

"As he paid for it by check, we can be positive of his identity then,'' the station chief said, but Dan made a wry face.

"That's hardly necessary; it would appear that Mr. Shirafuji made a habit of buying jewelry for pretty young women. He had visited the Southern Cross several times, each time with a different girl, and all the staff in the shop knew him on sight.''

"I see, so that answers the question of where the ring comes from, but how about the barb on the platinum?'' the station chief asked in an effort to hurry him on.

"I only took a picture of the ring with me when I was trying to trace the shop that sold it, but as soon as I was sure of this, I took the actual ring itself and showed it to them. The manager and several other members of the staff were able to confirm that it was the same one they had sold Mr. Shirafuji, but none of them had seen the barb protruding from the platinum like that before and they were all willing to swear that it had not been damaged in that way when they sold it. They did say, however, that it wouldn't be too difficult for a person to make a barb like that using a pair of pliers or something similar.''

"So that means that Shirafuji did it before he gave her the ring. . . .'' someone muttered.

"I don't agree,'' Dan replied with uncharacteristic haste. "If Mr. Shirafuji wanted to poison her with lysin in that manner, I think it very unlikely that he would do so with a ring that could be traced so easily to him. Anyway, if that was the case, she would have been poisoned the first time she wore the ring and yet she was seen to wear it at the company party last October without any ill effects. I suppose he could have worked on it after the party, though. . . .''

"I don't think that's very likely,'' one of the detectives from HQ said. "If he was going to do it at all, I think he would have done so from the beginning. Anyway, I agree that it's unlikely that the person who gave her the ring would be responsible.''

''That means that we will have to concentrate on who could have had access to the ring later on,'' the station chief added, then looked back to Dan.

''I think it was probably someone close to the victim or someone who had a chance to approach her. I think whoever it was must've stolen the ring from her house, made the barb, filled the space behind the pearl with lysin, and then returned it to her jewelry box. A black pearl is usually only worn on formal occasions or funerals, so it's quite likely that whoever killed her did the work in the time between Mr. Shirafuji's accident and his funeral two days later. I think they could've been quite sure that she'd wear the ring to his funeral.''

''Couldn't it have been done earlier?'' one of the younger detectives asked.

''Of course, that's quite possible. As far as we can tell, the lysin had been mixed in with an ointment of some kind and then sealed with wax; it could have lain in her jewelry box indefinitely without losing its potency. Once she put it on, the warmth of her hand, combined with the vibrations it would receive while it was being worn, would be sufficient to melt the wax and release the poison. If the murderer had no particular concern as to the time of her death, he could have rigged the ring whenever he had the opportunity and then waited patiently until she wore it.''

''Yes, but who could have had the opportunity to steal the ring and then return it without her noticing it missing? That is the question.''

''Certainly,'' Dan said. ''I asked Wakao to investigate her background. Maybe he'll be able to enlighten us.'' Dan handed over the floor to his subordinate.

''Of course,'' Wakao replied. ''This is what I managed to learn about the life of the deceased.

''Yaeko Ichihara had been living on her own at the house in Jiyugaoka for the last two years, ever since her son Hikaru married and moved to an apartment in Yakumo. She has a housekeeper, Tsune Shinozuka, sixty-five, of Todoroki, who comes to clean the house five days a week."

"She lives on her own? That makes it a bit . . ."

"Yes, that's right, it makes it very difficult for us to know much about her life-style. The company sent a car every morning to take her to work and Tsune came to the house Mondays to Fridays from 1:00 to 7:00 P.M. to do the cleaning and laundry, and, if it was necessary, she also made preparations for the evening meal.

"I asked her to tell me as much as she knew about Yaeko's private life, and one thing both she and the son agreed on was that she liked to invite people back to her house for a meal regularly. This was not only on weekends; on weekdays, too, she'd often invite business associates back for drinks and conversation. Tsune said she would often arrive to find things left as they had been the previous night, and the son, Hikaru, said that he sometimes called during weekends to find his mother out and a pile of dirty dishes in the kitchen. So I'm afraid that we have a situation in which a regular stream of people was flowing in and out of the house."

"We'll have to check on all her acquaintances then."

"That's correct, but while I was talking to her, I learned something very interesting from Tsune." Wakao paused for a moment until he was sure that he had everyone's attention, then continued.

"First, on the afternoon of April 29, which was a holiday, she went to the house as usual, to find Yaeko in bed. She had heard that she would be going to Atami the previous day to attend the wedding of a friend's daughter and that she'd be spending the night there, so she guessed that Yaeko must have been exhausted when she got home and had gone right to bed. She started to tidy up the living room when Yaeko got up and told her a strange thing.

"She said that one of the windows in her bedroom had been open and there were signs that someone had entered the room. The lock had been broken for some time, and even though she had known this was just asking for trouble, she'd just left it as it was. However, when she came home the previous night, she found that it had been removed altogether, and there seemed to be something strange about the room, as if someone had been in there. Both she and Tsune searched the room, but they couldn't find anything amiss, and Yaeko checked her jewelry box, but none of her rings were missing. As nothing appeared to have been stolen, she guessed that her imagination had been playing tricks on her and didn't bother to call us in, but the next day she contacted a locksmith and had him come in to install a new lock.''

Wakao looked around the room to see how the others had taken his news before he went on.

''There's something else, too. When Tsune was cleaning the bedroom one day, she found a thick, black, man's fountain pen under the bed. This was a few days after the twenty-ninth, but she couldn't be sure how long it had been lying there. However, the carpet in the bedroom had been relaid at the end of February this year and so we can be certain that it was dropped sometime after that. She picked the pen up, and when she studied it, she noticed a name engraved on it.''

He paused and looked around the room again, enjoying the effect his news was having on the rest of the investigation team.

''The name was Okito Shirafuji.''

4

The White Powder

I

"Toko! Toko!"

Toko was walking through the campus grounds when she heard her name called. She stopped and turned back to see Akira hurrying toward her. He was wearing a sport shirt and jeans and had, as usual, a thin notebook tucked under his arm.

He was quite tall, and long-legged, and she had often thought that if he took a little more trouble about his appearance, he would be quite good-looking, but today she found his appearance strangely reassuring. She stood and waited until he reached her.

"Toko, how have you been? I was worried about you." He frowned and looked at her face carefully. "You didn't call, so I guessed you must be busy."

It was the first time Toko had seen him since the day they had heard of Ryuta's accident as they were hurrying back

71

from Disneyland. He had phoned her every other day since then, but she had often been out.

"I'm sorry, the day before yesterday at Jiyugaoka—"

She was about to tell him that she had meant to phone him from the phone booth there, but then she remembered that she had hung up on him without saying a word and suddenly broke off in midsentence. Although she did not like to keep secrets from him, she was not sure how she should explain the way she had acted that day.

Akira did not seem to notice that she had not finished her sentence. "Is Yaeko Ichihara's funeral finished?" he asked.

"Yes, they held the service at the temple yesterday."

"So you're over the worst of it now, then?"

"Yes, but this time it was murder, and they still have no idea who could have done it."

Akira saw how depressed she was, and glancing down at his watch, he said, "Do you have any classes now?"

"No, I just finished."

Her linguistics lecture had ended at 2:45 and she had nothing else scheduled for the day.

"Let's go and have a cup of coffee somewhere then," he suggested.

"Okay."

The early-summer sun flooded the campus, and being late afternoon, it was very quiet, with only an occasional shout coming from the direction of the playing fields.

"Does that mean that you have detectives coming around questioning you?" Akira asked as they walked.

"Yes, they came around yesterday, and I was asked all kinds of things at the funeral, too. Father says that they are in and out of the company offices all the time."

"What kinds of things do they ask you?"

"They mostly ask me questions about what happened when Yaeko collapsed, but they asked my mother who Yaeko had been seeing these days."

"The papers say that the murderer was probably someone who was quite close to her."

"Yes, they think that her ring was stolen and the poison put into it and then returned to her jewel case."

"Where did she keep her jewel case?"

"In a cupboard in her bedroom—apparently she didn't use a safe. That's why they think it must be someone close to her. Whoever it was, they had to be able to get into her bedroom and had to know where she kept her jewelry."

"Shall we go to Erica's?" Akira asked.

As they left the main gate of the school, he suggested the name of one of the local coffee shops and the two of them walked down the tree-lined street.

"The simplest solution would be if it were one of her family or her housekeeper," Akira said, returning to the subject of the murder. "Any of them would have had ample opportunity."

"Yes, but she always had people coming around to visit her at her home. She was a very talkative, gregarious person and she probably found it terribly lonely to live on her own like that."

Toko had always found Yaeko to be very beautiful in a cold sort of way, and although she had often found her scathing tongue almost unbearable, she realized now just what a sad figure Yaeko had been.

"I wonder when the poison was first put into the ring," Akira said, interrupting her thoughts.

"They seem to think that that is the key to the case. In fact . . ." Toko found it difficult to go on. The previous night one of the detectives had come to her family's house and sown a seed of doubt in her mind; ever since, she had felt very depressed. She knew that she should not talk about it, but felt she could trust Akira. "Listen, this is still being kept secret from the press, but last night a detective came to see mother and asked her about Uncle Okito."

They turned into the road where the coffee shop was located and then came to a stop, facing each other.

"He wanted to know if Uncle Okito and Yaeko had become close again before he died—like they used to be in the old days."

"What is it that the police are hiding from the press?"

"A pen belonging to Okito was found under Yaeko's bed."

"When?"

"The housemaid found it in May, but a new carpet had been installed in February, so it would have to have been sometime after that. The carpet was laid at the end of February, twenty days before Okito died."

"Is that pen still at Yaeko's house?"

"No, the maid said she didn't say anything when she found it, she just put it on the side table, but no matter how the police searched, they could find no trace of it."

"I suppose that means that Yaeko must have returned it to Okito," Akira theorized.

"Yes, that's the most natural explanation, and the detective seemed to think so, too. That means that Okito and Yaeko must have met at least twice before he died—once when he dropped his pen under her bed, and once when she returned it to him. There was something else strange, too. Yaeko had said that she thought a burglar had broken in on the twenty-eighth of April, but there was nothing missing, so the police seem to think that she just imagined the whole thing."

The coffee shop was about thirty yards down the road from where they were standing; as they talked, the door opened to emit a glorious smell of freshly roasted coffee and four rather scruffy-looking students. They walked past Toko and Akira and disappeared in the direction of the college.

"Anyway, let's have a cup of coffee," Akira said.

"Yes, let's."

Toko liked to have Viennese coffee with plenty of cream in it, while Akira preferred mocha or Blue Mountain, although for some reason Blue Mountain cost one hundred and fifty yen more than the other types.

Akira slipped his arm around Toko's shoulders and they turned in the direction of the coffee shop.

At that moment a car horn sounded behind them and a thrill ran through Toko's body. In some mysterious way she knew instantly what type of car it was and who was driving.

She turned back, almost apprehensively, and saw the driver's powerful fingers tapping out a rhythm on the door of the Carrera. When their eyes met, the fingers stopped moving and Akihito nodded slightly toward her.

"I seemed to remember you saying that you went to college somewhere around here, so I thought I'd drive by and see what kind of place it was. I never dreamed I would actually run into you like this."

Toko felt her cheeks burning and looked from Akihito to Akira.

"This is Akira Takubo, he's a third-year student at the university, studying commercial science, and this is Akihito Shirafuji, my cousin; he's a potter." Akihito nodded to Akira with a friendly smile, but Toko did not see how Akira responded; she found herself unable to take her eyes off Akihito's face. "What are you doing today?"

"I thought I'd drive out to the house at Egota. Actually, I called my hotel a short while ago and found that I had a message from the Ogikubo police station asking me to get in touch with them as soon as possible. It's all very exciting, isn't it?"

"Has something else happened?" Toko asked.

"No, not that I know of." Akihito's face creased into a smile. "When I called them back, they said that they would like to search the house at Egota if I didn't object, and they would like me to be there to witness it."

"Your father's house? Why?"

"I'm not sure, they gave me all kinds of reasons, but I don't have any reason to refuse them. If it clears up all the suspicion surrounding his death, I would be more than happy to oblige."

Toko nodded in agreement.

"Anyway, I'm on my way over there now, and it occurred to me that it might be useful if you were to come, too."

"Useful? In what way?"

"The house is still more or less the way he left it, and though I've made a start on cleaning it up, I've been away for so long now that I'm not sure where everything is. I don't know how my father spent his last years or what things were important to him, so I wouldn't be able to answer the police if they questioned me. That's why I thought if you were there . . .''

But I don't know anything about his house either, Toko thought, but to her amazement, she found herself saying, "Yes, I'd love to go. I'd like to see Uncle Okito's house one more time. You say that it's just as he left it . . . ?''

II

I am sorry, Akira, but you see how it is, she murmured to herself as she watched his tall figure shrink in the rearview mirror of the car. She was sure that he would realize that she had no choice, what with the police searching Okito's house like that, and she hoped he would forgive her. He was always very understanding and she felt sure that he would appreciate her dilemma; she just did not want to hurt him. But it was strange, if she really had no choice but to go with Akihito, why should she feel so guilty about it?

When Akira disappeared from the mirror, she turned to Akihito.

"Thank you for showing me such a lovely time the other night." She did her utmost to sound very grown-up.

"Actually I went back to the hotel after I saw you home. I enjoyed our evening together so much that I didn't want it to end so quickly, and I have been staying there ever since.''

"How about Egota?''

"As I said just now, I've hardly started to clean it up yet, and a French potter I know is holding a show of his work in Ginza starting this week, so I'll have to help him out, too.''

I wonder how long Akihito is going to stay in Japan? she thought, and a chill seemed to pass through her body.

"Have you heard about the fountain pen they found?'' Akihito asked as they drove along Mejiro Avenue.

"Yes, do you think that the police are hoping to find that at the house in Egota?''

"Yes, maybe, but I think they may be looking for something else entirely."

The house was built in a quiet residential area a short distance from the northern exit to Egota Station. It was a traditional, two-story building; the garden was rather overgrown. There was no garage, and Akihito could only just manage to fit the car into the driveway between the gate and the front door.

"It doesn't look as if they've arrived yet," he said as he took the key out of his pocket and opened the front door.

Ryuta's house contained a unique smell that could be called the very essence of Ryuta, and in the same way, Okito's house also had its own scent, which brought back thousands of memories to Toko. Akihito drew the curtains in the hall and threw open all the windows to let in a cool, evening spring breeze.

"Did you often come here to play?" he asked.

"Only until about the time I graduated high school, but how about you? Did you live here?"

"Father moved here the winter after my mother died. I spent a lot of time at my grandparents' house in Toshimaen at the time and so he moved here from Mejiro to be near me."

"It must have lots of memories for you then."

"Yeah, I lived here for five years before I went to America, but it was very lonely after my mother died; my father never came home from the laboratory until late, and I had to wait up on my own. But you're right, it does have memories for me."

"Yes, for me too."

This was another point on which they both agreed.

He started to show her around the house. On the first floor there were two adjoining living rooms, a reception room with French windows, a small Japanese-style room that Okito had used as a bedroom, a dressing room, and a maid's room. On the second floor there were two Japanese-style rooms and one Western-style room, which he had obviously used as study workrooms since all three were piled high with books and papers.

Toko and Akihito were not allowed very much time to their memories, for they were immediately interrupted by a loud, uncouth voice calling from the front door.

"I'm from the Ogikubo police station," the man shouted after Akihito answered him.

They hurried downstairs to find four men, who had already taken off their shoes and were standing in the hall. One was wearing a suit, but the other three were in overalls. All of them were wearing gloves.

"I am very sorry to bother you, like this," said Wakao, who was the one in the suit. He looked over at Toko in surprise; he had met her when he was investigating Yaeko's death, so he know who she was.

The police split into two groups, one going upstairs to start their search while Wakao and the remaining man moved into the reception room. Akihito went up to the second floor to keep an eye on the men there, and Toko followed Wakao into the reception room.

They went through all the drawers and even checked behind the mantelpiece clock, then they moved through the living rooms and finally started to work on the bedroom. They opened a door to reveal a small closet that Toko had not noticed before. It was piled high with books, prototypes of various calculators, and parts of machines. The detective in overalls squeezed into the open space and started to check each of the items carefully.

There were several old photograph albums, which the detective put to one side, then, moving a pile of books, he found a small hidden cabinet. Even Toko, who was looking on from a distance, thought it a strange place to keep a cabinet. The man opened the door and found four medicine bottles about four inches high, which he brought out and placed on the table in front of Wakao.

Three of the bottles were almost empty. Their contents had dried up and were stuck to the inside of the glass, but the fourth contained a small amount of white powder, and when Wakao shook it, it moved. He opened the lid and sniffed, then gave a shrug. He turned to the other man.

"Go and get him," he said.

The man in overalls nodded and hurried upstairs. He returned almost immediately with Akihito in tow.

"Mr. Shirafuji, do you have any idea what the contents of this bottle are?" Wakao asked.

"Where did you find it?"

"There was a small cabinet hidden behind the books in there and this bottle was inside."

"What, in there?" Akihito looked in at the cabinet as if it were the first time he had ever seen it. "I'm sorry, but I never noticed the cabinet before; I haven't gotten around to cleaning up this room yet."

"And I take it that you didn't know anything about it either, Miss Chino?"

"That is correct."

Akihito looked quite pale and was not able to take his eyes off the bottle.

"There's probably no need to worry, it could quite easily be insect repellent, but I'm afraid I don't know how to tell the difference."

III

The police investigators spent three hours searching the house, but were unable to find the fountain pen. They finally went away, taking with them the four bottles they had found in the cabinet in the closet.

After their departure, Akihito and Toko both felt exhausted and sat down in the reception room. Outside, night had fallen.

"They went through all the notes and plans they found on the second floor, but those all refer to my father's research, so they couldn't make much sense of them. They didn't even bother to ask if I knew what they were about."

"The problem is just those bottles, then," Toko surmised.

On the way over in the car, Akihito had hinted that the

police might be looking for something more than just the pen, but surely not . . .

"Surely that bottle couldn't have contained . . ." Toko began, voicing her thoughts.

Akihito shook his head and gave her a reassuring smile. Although he had half expected the police to find something like that, he could not believe it when they did. He looked up at the clock; it was 6:50.

"What would you say to having dinner somewhere and forgetting all about it?"

"Yes, I'd love to, but first there's something I'd like to see, if you don't mind."

"What is that?"

"Uncle Okito's photograph albums. I noticed four or five of them in the closet when the police were searching it. I thought there might be a picture in one of them of that person."

"Which person?"

"The one I told you about the other night over dinner."

Akihito soon realized who she was referring to.

"Oh, you mean the woman who was with my father when you met him in Ginza that time?"

"Yes."

She could still picture herself sitting in the club in Ginza with them and Okito taking the woman's hand and saying, *This person is going to go far away from me, Toko, but our hearts will remain together forever.* It had made a tremendous impression on her at the time; she guessed that she had not been ready to hear things like that when she was so young.

Although Okito had been an electronics genius, he had also enjoyed reading the classics, and sometimes he would come out with some very romantic lines. That night in Ginza, he had been very drunk, but despite this, Toko felt convinced that he had spoken to her straight from his heart.

"I hope you will not think me rude when I say this. . . ."

She spoke in a much more adult manner than she was accustomed to. This might have been because Akihito was much older than her university friends and she just naturally changed her way of speaking to match his, or perhaps she was trying to make herself look her best. Even she could not be sure which it was.

"Your parents were married while they were still in college and your father never remarried after your mother died."

"Yes."

"Well, although he never remarried, he knew a lot of women. . . ."

"There's no need to try and spare my feelings," Akihito said with a smile. "I know that my father became a real playboy and had a different woman virtually every night. There are certain people who seem to enjoy making sure that I get to hear all the unsavory gossip about him."

"Well, supposing that among all the women he knew, there was one that he really loved and that was the person I met that night in Ginza. Maybe he wanted me to remember her as somebody special."

"If that is the case, then I'd like to meet her, too," Akihito said quietly. "You said that it was when you were about fifteen, which would make it about five and a half years ago. I was in New York at that time and so I had no way of knowing about it."

"I can remember her face quite clearly and I'm sure I'd be able to recognize her again if I saw her picture."

"Well, I hope that you'll be able to find one, but even if you can't, I'd appreciate it if you could go through the album with me and tell me what my father was like."

He stood up and put his hand gently over Toko's, then the two of them walked across the dimly lit room toward the bedroom.

During his lifetime, Okito had spread his futons here to sleep; on the morning of March 26, it was in this room that the housekeeper who came in every other day had found him dead. At that time, the room had been littered with whiskey bottles, glasses, bottles of sleeping pills, ashtrays piled high with cigarette butts, and scraps of paper with notes jotted on them that would mean nothing to an ordinary person. Of course that had all been cleared away now, and an old, large, rosewood table stood where the bed had been, covered with a light film of dust.

Although she had not seen his body herself, Toko could imagine it as vividly as if she had and she shrank back for a moment.

"This is all of them," Akihito said, returning from the closet with four albums in his arms. "I've already had a look through them once."

The first one covered Okito's own childhood; it contained several pictures of his parents and Ryuta or Koji as children.

The second one was devoted to his wedding. He had been in his second year of college when he married another student, three years his senior, whom he had been dating since his first year. Akihito had been born later the same year; Toko remembered Ryuta making a joke about it, saying that there had been a terrible rush to get the wedding over with before the child was born. When she looked at the pictures of the bride, she noticed that her stomach did appear to be a little swollen.

"Your mother was very beautiful, wasn't she?" she said with feeling. The woman in the photographs had had a very beautiful profile and her eyes seemed to sparkle.

For the first three years of his life, the pictures of Akihito had been neatly pasted in with the date written next to them, but after that, things began to fall into disarray. They came across several pictures from the time when Okito had worked as a lab assistant at the university—at least he was standing in a large laboratory somewhere with an old man who was probably a professor and was working on something.

Among these pictures, there was one of him standing in the campus surrounded by four girl students; when Toko looked at their faces, she felt a shock of recognition. She concentrated on the student on the far right.

"It looks like her . . . yes, I'm pretty sure I'm right, that is the woman."

Akihito looked closer at the picture. "But isn't she a little young?"

"No, you must remember that I didn't meet her until much

later. Uncle Okito was forty-two, and I think the woman looked about thirty-five or six. If this is right, the ages would fit perfectly, wouldn't they? Uncle Okito worked at the university for one year after he got his master's degree, so that would make him twenty-five and the girl could easily have been a first-year student.''

"Yes, and as an assistant, he would be quite likely to have taken over some of the classes.''

The girl in the pictures had a rather plump, round face with sparkling eyes. She had well-shaped lips from which large front teeth protruded slightly, giving her a very healthy, fresh look.

"I doubt that her face would change very much by the time she reached her midthirties; no, I think we can be sure that this is the woman I saw." As she was speaking, Toko suddenly realized that the woman looked somewhat similar to Akihito's mother.

"In that case," Akihito quickly replied, "we may be able to find more pictures of her."

His interest apparently piqued, Akihito started to look through the rest of the album. As he worked his way toward the end, the pictures became more and more disorganized, a lot of them merely tucked in between the pages.

There were pictures of Okito leaning against a hostess in a club or bar, pictures at various hotels with different women, a picture of him standing in front of a car with a woman. . . . It was easy to see that he had had a large number of lovers over the years, but to Toko's surprise, there was not a single picture of the woman she had met in Ginza.

"Maybe they weren't so close after all."

"Do you think so? I seem to get the opposite impression."

"What do you mean?"

"Maybe he was so serious about her that he didn't want to treat her like the other women." Toko felt that in the brief time period since she first met Akihito, she had grown up a great deal. "If he met her when he was still working at the university, it would mean that your mother was still alive, wouldn't it?"

"Yes, my mother died when father was thirty." Akihito didn't see the connection.

"In that case, I think we can be sure that there was nothing between them until then." She was not just being polite, she felt that Okito had really loved his wife and that was why he had never remarried. "Supposing they just bumped into each other after your mother died and had gradually fallen in love with each other. For some reason, however, the woman had to go away somewhere and that night I met them in Ginza had been their last night together. That would explain why he spoke to me as he did. . . ."

She could feel Akihito's gaze on her, and for some reason she felt as if it were Okito looking at her over his glass again.

Maybe, she thought, I was more than a little in love with Uncle Okito myself and the reason I never forgot the woman was because I was jealous of her.

Akihito reached out and touched her cheek, his hand moving around to her ear, and then down to her cheek. He leaned forward and his lips brushed her forehead.

Almost as if he kissed me, Toko thought, so quick and gently had the action been.

IV

A little after noon on Wednesday, May 20, the day after the search of Okito's house, Inspector Wakao returned from the university at Shinanomachi.

The station chief, Inspectors Dan, Yamaguchi, and Yuhara from HQ, and several of the other detectives involved in the investigation gathered together in one of the rooms of the Ogikubo station to hear his report.

"The analysis of the powder was completed on schedule," Wakao said, taking the bottle containing the white powder out of a large envelope he was carrying and putting it down on the table in front of him.

After finding the bottle at Okito's house, Wakao telephoned the investigation headquarters, and when he heard the report, Dan immediately got in touch with Professor Kawakita, who had performed the autopsy on Yaeko and taught forensic science at the university. When he heard the news, the professor asked to have Wakao bring the bottle to him for analysis.

"The professor of biochemistry came to the university this morning, so we asked him to run the analysis in his laboratory and the results are . . ." As usual, Wakao paused for effect and looked around his audience.

"Well, what did he say?" Yuhara prompted.

"The results are just what we expected—the bottle contained lysin."

He paused again and this time he was rewarded by sighs from his audience.

"I see, but where exactly does that leave us?" the station chief asked, staring into the bottle.

"I think that it's quite clear. This possibility was suggested earlier in the case, and the search of Okito Shirafuji's house was made in order to try and provide some concrete evidence to back it up. Thus, I think we can no longer afford to ignore this line of investigation." Wakao lost no time in putting forward his own theory. "Contrary to the usual pattern, where the murderer is hiding among the living, I think we must check the possibility that this murder was plotted by a dead man before he died. Of course, I am talking about Okito Shirafuji, who died on the twenty-fourth of March this year."

"Yes, and we could never be sure whether he died naturally or whether it was suicide," the station chief put in.

"The autopsy said that he died from cardiac arrest brought on by regular use of alcohol and barbiturates, but he was an academic and could quite easily have known just exactly how much more he needed to take before it would kill him," Wakao said.

"Some of the papers described it as a case of unprovable suicide," the station chief said.

"You mean that he set his trap before committing suicide?" Wakao asked. "He certainly had cause to feel betrayed by Yaeko Ichihara. She started off as his lover, but as soon as he started to lose favor at the company, she started a relationship with Ryuta and even managed to get herself named as a managing director. When Okito asked for more research funds, she was the first to oppose it.''

"Just a minute, let me get this straight," Yuhara said in an effort to bring their thoughts together. "We are to presume that Okito Shirafuji pretended to get close to Yaeko Ichihara again before he died in order to get the chance to visit her house and steal the black pearl ring.

"When he got the ring home, he hid the poison behind the pearl and formed the barb, then visited Ms. Ichihara's house again and returned the ring to her jewel case. However, during one of these visits, he accidentally dropped his fountain pen under the bed. Not knowing anything about any of this, the Ichihara woman wore the ring to Ryuta Shirafuji's funeral. . . .''

"There was Okito's funeral before that; she could easily have worn it to that,'' the station chief put in.

"Yes, but she was given the ring by Ryuta,'' one of the other detectives argued. "She may have been very thick-skinned, but she couldn't have really worn it to Okito's funeral, especially as everybody knew who bought it for her.''

"I don't think we need worry about that very much,'' Wakao said. "The murderer did not really care when she died. If she were to have worn the ring to his funeral, it would have been all the same to him, in fact he may even have thought that it would be a kind of poetic justice if she did. Either way, he wouldn't care when she put the ring on just as long as the poison did its trick.''

"That's true,'' Dan said slowly. "If the murderer really was Okito, he wouldn't be in any condition to worry about when she actually wore the ring.''

"Anyway, we found this lysin in Okito's home and we have evidence that would indicate that Okito visited Ichihara's house a short while before his death, so even if we can't prove it yet, I think it's safe to say that he is the most likely suspect we have to date. I remember someone the other day remarking that it was a very roundabout way of killing someone, but if Okito wanted to kill someone after he himself had died, it would have to be a roundabout way.''

''But how about a motive?'' asked the station chief.

''As I said just now, I think that it's quite easy to see why he might have a grudge against her.''

''But why just her?'' Dan murmured suddenly.

''What?''

''Surely he'd have had a grudge against all the heads of Ruco. After all, it was due to his inventions like the SuperMini that the company grew as it did, and while they were very nice to him when things were going well, as soon as he had trouble with his research they cast him aside and forced him into the lonely existence of his last days. I know that this may not be totally true, but he could easily have thought it was.''

''Who do you mean by the heads of Ruco?'' the chief asked.

''Well, there's Ryuta and Koji Shirafuji, and Yaeko Ichihara, of course. I suppose you could add Hiroshi Chino to that list, too.''

''But Ryuta is already dead, so—''

''Yes, and he died *after* Okito,'' Dan said, interrupting the chief. All eyes in the room turned toward him.

''You can't mean that Ryuta Shirafuji's death was more than an accident,'' the chief exclaimed.

''If we're going to accept Wakao's theory, it would look that way.''

The chief stood mulling this over.

A new tension filled the room and they all tried to remember as many details as they could about the crash. They had become so involved in Yaeko's death that Ryuta's accident seemed to have taken place a long time ago when in fact only one week had passed.

''What did the crash investigators report? Does anyone know?'' the chief asked.

''The papers say that they still consider it to have been caused by condensation in the fuel tanks,'' Yuhara replied.

''They haven't released their report yet then?''

"No, if I remember correctly, the crash investigation committee has to hand in an official report to the transport minister, but that's not for another six months yet," Yuhara said.

"So they don't give a report before then, do they?" Yamaguchi asked.

"The investigation team is based at the Five Lakes station, aren't they?" Wakao asked.

"Yes, it's only a week since the crash, so I think they will still be working on it down there. That's where we will probably get the most up-to-date information," Yuhara said.

"Should we get in touch with them?" Wakao asked, looking over at the station chief.

"Yes, you call them, Dan."

"Yes, sir."

One of the younger detectives looked up the number and passed it to Dan. He dialed it, and when someone answered at the other end, he introduced himself and asked to speak to the officer in charge of the crash investigation. He waited for a short while and then a deep, gruff voice came on the line.

"Hello, sorry to keep you waiting, Station Chief Nakazato here."

Dan had read about the crash in the scandal magazines and remembered that Nakazato was the first to arrive at the scene of the accident. A brief story about Nakazato had appeared in one magazine that mentioned him as the man who had been responsible for solving the murder of the chairman of Wada Pharmaceuticals.

"They finished their investigations here in about three days and have gone back to Tokyo to analyze their findings. I'm afraid that there are no experts left here now who could help you."

"That's all right, but we would be very grateful if you could tell us what their findings are to date."

"You mean there could be a connection between the crash and the death of Yaeko Ichihara?"

When Nakazato had heard where they were calling from, it did not take him very long to put two and two together.

"Yes," Dan replied. "To be quite honest, we feel there's a possibility that the poison found in the victim's ring could have been put there before Okito Shirafuji died, and if that is the case, we wondered if someone could have done something to cause Ryuta Shirafuji's plane to crash."

"I see," Nakazato answered in the same calm voice. "Well, at the moment the crash is thought to have been due to an engine failure caused by condensation in the fuel tanks. The pilot raised this possibility in his communication with the ground, and even if he hadn't, it's the most common cause of sudden engine failure soon after takeoff."

"I see, and what causes this condensation?" Dan asked.

"It forms when the tank is not completely filled and the moisture in the air condenses to water. The pilot is supposed to check for this by opening a petcock under the main tank, but you'd be surprised how many people don't bother to do so. Most pilots fill their tanks immediately on landing so that there's no room for air to enter and subsequently no fear of condensation. For this reason they don't bother to look for it during their preflight checks. Later investigations proved that Ryuta Shirafuji was one of these pilots."

"You mean he didn't check his tanks?"

"Yes, we learned from other pilots at Chofu Airfield that he usually took off without bothering to check."

"But if, as you say, he always had the fuel tank filled as soon as he landed, there would be no room for the water to build up."

"Yes, that's true; there could be a number of reasons why it happened, but the investigation team has yet to release its findings."

"Could you tell us your thoughts on it?"

"Mmm . . ." Nakazato was silent for a short while. "One answer could be that he neglected to fill the tanks after his last flight, but that has already been refuted. His last flight was approximately two months ago, from ten to twelve in the morning of the fourteenth of March, and when he finished, he went straight to the fuel depot and had the tanks filled. We know this from the receipts at the depot."

"Saturday the fourteenth of March . . ." That was ten days before Okito's death, Dan thought. "But if he definitely filled the tank, how could there have been a buildup of condensation like that?"

"Apparently there was no trace of a leak, so we can only assume that the tanks weren't filled quite to the brim at the fuel depot. A lot of pilots check this themselves just to make sure, but apparently Mr. Shirafuji never bothered. He was a rather happy-go-lucky type. He probably checked the fuel gauges before he took off, but if it was only a small space, they would have still indicated full. Unfortunately, there's no way we can find that out now."

Dan paused for a moment before responding, then made up his mind to ask the question that had been bothering him from the beginning. "I don't suppose there's any suspicion that it was not an accident and someone might have tampered with the plane sometime between Ryuta's last flight in March and this one? Apparently the plane was kept in the open, so there was ample opportunity for anyone to approach it unhindered, but would it be possible for them to cause the engine to stop like that? I'm afraid that I am a complete amateur when it comes to aircraft."

"Me too," Nakazato said with a laugh, "but . . ."

"But what?"

"I must stress that the accident board has yet to issue its report, but I did ask the chief investigator whether it would have been possible for someone to cause the plane to crash like that on purpose."

"And what did he say?"

"He said that technically, it was quite possible."

"What would they have to do?"

"It's quite simple, all they'd have to do is drain a cupful of gasoline from the main tank and replace it with a cupful of water. If this was done, the gauges would still indicate that the tank was full."

Dan paused for a moment as he thought this over. "Thank you very much," he said with feeling. He was about to replace the receiver when Nakazato spoke.

"You said your name was Dan, didn't you?"

"Yes, sir."

"Just now you mentioned that there was a possibility that the poison in Yaeko Ichihara's ring had been put there before Okito Shirafuji died. What led you to think so?"

"When we searched Okito Shirafuji's house yesterday, we found a small bottle hidden in a closet that contained a white powder, and when we had it analyzed, it proved to be lysin."

He replied without a moment's hesitation. They intended to keep this fact a secret from the press for the moment, but he knew that there was no chance of Nakazato letting it slip.

"I see, so there was some lysin hidden in Okito's house."

"That is correct."

"And you think that he may have put the poison in Yaeko Ichihara's ring and tampered with Ryuta Shirafuji's plane before he died?"

"Yes, don't you agree?"

"Yes, I suppose if I was in your situation, I would think the same, but I feel there's something wrong with it somewhere."

"What precisely?"

"It seems bizarre to me that you would find the poison at Okito's house like that."

5

The Woman by the Lake

I

THERE IS A HILL IN THE MOTO-AZABU AREA OF TOKYO
which is known as *Kurayamizaka*, which means "the pitch-
black hill." It is very steep, and near the top there is a very
attractive little tea room.

There are a large number of foreign embassies in the area
and the streets are lined with rather forbidding, foreign-style
houses for the diplomats, but the tea room, sandwiched between one brick and one stone building, looks just like an
ordinary house. It is set back a short distance from the road,
and the walls to its pointed roof are covered with ivy, making
it look like something from a fairy tale.

On the day that Toko hurried toward it, the black Porsche
was already standing in the lot outside, and she felt a thrill
pass through her body upon noticing it there.

Inside the floor was made of beautifully polished teak and
Vivaldi's *Four Seasons* was playing softly in the background.
It was a little after three on a cloudy weekday afternoon and

there were very few customers. Akihito was sitting alone at a table near the back and he waved to her as she walked in.

"I'm sorry I'm late."

"Did you get lost?"

"Not really."

"That's good. When I heard that you were going to Nishi-Azabu, I thought this would be a good place to meet since it's not too far away from there."

"How did you know about this place?" Toko asked.

"My friend from France, the one who's holding a show in Ginza, is staying near here with a French family, and I noticed this place on my way back from visiting him one night."

They fell silent and sat looking out of the window for a short while. There was hardly anyone on the street, just the occasional limousine that glided by without a sound. The waiter came with Akihito's coffee and asked Toko for her order. She asked for a Viennese coffee. After the waiter had gone away again, Akihito frowned slightly.

"I had a call from the police yesterday about the results of the search at the house the day before."

"What, do you mean about the powder being lysin?" Toko asked anxiously, but in a low voice, since this fact had yet to be made public.

"Yes, right, and last night a detective came to my hotel and asked me all kinds of questions."

"Surely they can't think that Uncle Okito would—"

"They can and do. They suspected him to begin with, that's why they made the search in the first place. They just found what they were looking for and confirmed their suspicions."

"But surely . . ." Toko began, repeating herself.

"Of course I don't believe that it could have been my father," Akihito said forcefully, in a low voice. "I could hardly believe it when I first heard that it was lysin in that bottle, but after I thought about it awhile, it convinced me that it couldn't have been my father who killed Yaeko."

Toko was genuinely puzzled. "What do you mean?"

"If he had planned to get his revenge on Yaeko after he died, he would never have left the evidence lying around like that, asking to be found. He would have thrown the remainder away after he had put the poison inside the ring."

Suddenly this seemed the only possibility to Toko, and she said, "Yes, I agree."

"You read about how murderers leave clues to their identity on purpose, and one could say that my father left the poison in the house on purpose to advertise what he had done, but I don't think he was that kind of a man. If he was going to do something like that, I think he'd have made his death an obvious suicide and hinted at his revenge in a suicide note."

"I agree. I think he couldn't stand the thought of people saying that he committed suicide because he couldn't continue his research. He could never admit defeat like that, his pride wouldn't allow him to, and if he wanted revenge—"

Toko broke off hurriedly, thinking that she might have said too much, but to her relief, Akihito nodded in agreement.

"That's right. If my father was planning revenge, he would do it in a way that would make it impossible to prove afterward. He might leave a clue as to the identity of the culprit, but he'd make sure that nobody could ever be certain. He would commit a perfect crime; he was clever enough to do it if he put his mind to it. He wouldn't leave the poison lying around to be found in a simple search like that."

He broke off as the waiter came with Toko's coffee and they both sat in silence until he went away again.

"How did the poison get there, I wonder," Toko murmured into her coffee.

"Someone must have put it there," Akihito replied simply. "I don't think it just happened to be there; my father never studied poisons." After pausing for a moment, he added, "Any number of people have been in and out of the house recently for the funeral and memorial services, and anyway, as you know, that house is becoming a bit decrepit now and it wouldn't be difficult for someone to get inside while it was empty."

"I agree, someone must have crept in and left the lysin there to be found later, but why would they go to the trouble?"

"Well, the most obvious reason would be that they wanted to kill Yaeko and pin the blame on my father."

"If that's so, do you think that Uncle Ryuta's crash was really an accident?''

Akihito had told her that the police were beginning to suspect foul play in connection with Ryuta's plane crash when he telephoned her the day before.

"I don't know, perhaps—"

"Perhaps somebody is getting revenge for Uncle Okito's death and he wants everybody else to know why he is doing it.''

Akihito gave a gasp of surprise and looked up at Toko. "Why do you say that?"

"I don't know. Do you remember me telling you about that dream I had of Uncle Okito the night before Uncle Ryuta died? He said, 'Watch me, Toko. I've got a present for all of them. I'll send them all death from here on top of the clouds.'

"I feel that Uncle might really have felt that way and he contacted me by telepathy.''

"There is another possible explanation," Akihito suggested. "Perhaps *you* believed that my father had been wronged and wanted revenge; that would explain why you saw that dream.''

"Yes, that's true," Toko admitted. "But they say that dead people often appear in dreams to people close to them, and it occurred to me that Uncle may have appeared in somebody else's dream as well. Someone who loved him very much . . . like Reika Asai. I'm sure he must have told her something.''

"Reika Asai?"

"Yes, that girl student.''

"How do you know her name?" Akihito exclaimed loudly, and the other people in the coffee bar looked over at him.

"When you told me that the white powder the police found was lysin, I decided to find out who she was. I knew from the picture we saw in the album that she was probably a student when Okito was working at the university in 1964, and so it wasn't too difficult to find out the rest."

The university Okito had attended was situated in Azabu, and so Toko had visited the library there and gone through all the yearbooks. She knew that the woman had been a student in 1964, so she decided to go through the yearbooks from 1965 to 1968. The students were all listed according to their majors, and there was a photograph of each, so it did not take her long to find what she was looking for.

"I guessed that she would have studied science if she were to meet Uncle Okito, and sure enough, she graduated with a major in chemistry in 1967."

"That was lucky. She must have been very clever to graduate in a subject like that, but there's no telling what's happened to her now."

"Yes, I thought that it would be a hopeless task, but it proved to be remarkably easy."

Akihito was amazed. "What, you mean you checked with the Old Boy club?"

"Yes, most colleges are the same, they have a special section that keeps records of the OB's, and they're usually willing to supply general information like a person's name and address to an outsider if they are asked to."

"Did you find out where she's living now?"

"Yes, they had a record of her home and work addresses. They send out postcards every three years to check that their information is up to date." Toko took out her pocket diary. "Oh yes, she's called Reika Terauchi now, so I think she must have married. Her present address is Lake Kawaguchi Town in Yamanashi prefecture."

"Lake Kawaguchi? That name brings back memories; I remember going there on a school outing when I was in junior high school. I suppose that this Reika must have married someone from there."

"I don't know if she moved there straight from Tokyo, though. . . ."

When she had met Reika in Ginza six years earlier, in

1981, Okito had talked of her going away somewhere. As Toko had been told that the list of names was revised every three years, she asked if she could see the previous list.

"In the list before that, which was drawn up in 1981, she is listed under her maiden name and her address is in Shimo-Ochiai, which is quite near Egota. It also said that she worked for Toyo Oil."

"So she was an office worker."

"Yes, I think so. She probably got married in the autumn of the year I saw her and moved to Lake Kawaguchi."

"So she graduated from the university in 1967, went to work for Toyo Oil, and then married in 1981."

"Yes, she didn't marry until she was thirty-six, which was about the age I thought she was when I met her in Ginza, but I wonder why she waited so long to marry? She was very beautiful."

"I suppose she must have had her reasons."

Toko was convinced that she knew the reason and that the reason was that Reika had been having an affair with Okito.

"One thing worries me, however," Toko admitted. "What kind of thing do you think they make at Toyo Oil?"

"Judging by the name, I'd say that they probably make industrial and domestic oil products. You know, paints, things like that."

"That's what I mean."

"What?"

"Don't you remember? After Yaeko's death, that detective gave us a lecture on lysin and mentioned that castor oil is used in the manufacture of paint and that factories always have a large stock on hand."

Akihito gave another gasp and gave her a deep look. Until now, he had only thought of her as a young college girl, but he realized suddenly that he had sold her very short.

Yes, that's right, she thought as she looked back into his eyes. I have changed recently—ever since I first met you.

She felt as if she had woken up properly for the first time, that her sensitivity and intellect had reached new heights.

II

The following Saturday, Akihito turned up at Toko's house in Naka-Meguro at four o'clock in the afternoon. Her father, Hiroshi, was at work, and although he usually only worked a five-day week, the sudden death of the company president and one of the managing directors had left the Ruco Corporation in a state of crisis. As a result, both Hiroshi and the new president, Koji, were working day and night to try and come through it unscathed.

Akihito was shown through to the dining room, where Toko's mother, Sachiko, offered him a cup of tea and a slice of lemon pie.

"Are you still going to go? The weather doesn't look very good," Sachiko said, glancing out of the window.

The sky was overcast and the occasional gust of wind flung heavy raindrops against the window. It was so dark outside that some of the street lamps had come on already.

"Yes, it's a pity that we couldn't have gone earlier, but my friend's exhibition at Ginza lasted until today and I couldn't get away until now."

"Tomorrow I've got to go to Miko's wedding, so that's out," Toko added, referring to a friend from high school who was going to be married the next day.

"Next week I'm going to be rather busy, so I'm afraid that it will have to be today."

"I feel that I must meet Reika Asai—sorry, Terauchi—as soon as possible and then we can work out what to do after that."

Toko could not get her mind off the woman she had met that time in Ginza and would not be able to rest easy until she talked to her again. She had told her mother all about it, as she always found it helped to talk things over with her. She had not, however, told her about the change that had come over her since she met Akihito.

"In that case, you'd better get a move on or it will be late. It's very cold out today, so be careful."

Sachiko was very easygoing and did not make any comments about their plans or even appear to notice the way they were beginning to behave around each other, but she was also a very practical woman, and hurrying upstairs, she got a cardigan for each of them.

"Thank you very much," Akihito said with a wry smile as he accepted the one she offered him.

It was 4:30 by the time the Porsche pulled away from the curb outside Toko's home. The streets in town were crowded as usual, but once they got onto the expressway, they were able to speed up a little. They got occasional glimpses of the roofs of the tightly packed houses, and here and there large trees could be seen towering over the landscape, but under the gray sky, it all seemed strangely colorless.

"It will take us about two hours to get to Lake Kawaguchi at this rate, and by the time we find the house, it will probably be around seven o'clock," Akihito informed her.

"Yes, but that means that we're more likely to find her at home," Toko replied, undaunted.

Akihito nodded. They had both agreed that the best course would be for them to visit Reika like this, without any warning.

After they passed Lake Sagami, they entered Yamanashi prefecture and the road took them through several mountain passes. The sun was beginning to set now and the peaks of the mountains were lost in the clouds.

"If the weather had been better, we should have been able to see Mount Fuji from here," Toko said.

"Oh really? I have yet to see it since I got back to Japan. There's a very good picture of it in the lobby of the hotel, though, by Ryuzaburo Umehara."

They drove by Tsuru city, and as they passed the fields and simple farmhouses, Toko kept her eyes open since this was Akira Takubo's hometown. She had not spoken to him about today's excursion; in fact she had not seen him at college at all recently and she wondered what he was doing with himself.

They arrived at the Kawaguchi interchange at 6:45, which was about the time Akihito had predicted, and outside, the sky was almost totally black. He must have studied a map before he left because he turned off on Route 137 without any hesitation and headed toward the lake.

They soon arrived at the lakeside road, where they found a few small hotels and some souvenir shops. They came to a small coffee shop, and leaving the car in the parking lot opposite, they walked in.

"Are you feeling tired?" Akihito asked.

"Not really."

"How about food? Are you hungry?"

"No, not yet."

"Okay, we'll have a short rest here and then get on with it. I can ask directions to her house here."

Being a Saturday, the coffee shop was quite crowded, and after ordering two coffees, Akihito stood up and went over to the counter with a map of the area and the note he had made of Reika Terauchi's address. It did not take him long to find out what he needed, and he soon walked back to their table with a satisfied expression on his face.

"If we've got her address right, her house should be around here somewhere," he said, drawing a circle on the map between Routes 137 and 139. "There are some Toyo Oil company houses there, so I think that we're on the right track."

Toko was surprised. "You managed to find out all that?"

"Yes, the guy behind the counter lives near there, so he knows the area well. Actually, I didn't tell you before, but I called the company the other day and was able to find out that they have a laboratory on the eastern side of the lake, and there are some houses for the staff built within walking distance."

"Does that mean that Reika's husband—"

"Yes, I think it is likely that he works in the laboratory. She might have continued to work for the company after she married, but I didn't want to ask in case word got back to her that someone was checking up on her and she was put on her guard."

"Yes, I can't wait to see how she reacts when we mention Okito's name to her."

They finished their coffee and hurried over to the car. They drove back along Route 137 until they reached a turnoff heading in the right direction. It was quite dark outside now and there were only the occasional cluster of houses surrounded by fields or open space.

"The guy in the coffee shop said it's in a row of five or six terraced houses."

They drove around in circles, sometimes coming back to the place they started from, but Akihito did not give up. Toko thought that it would be much quicker if they were to ask somebody, but she kept quiet. She knew that men did not like to ask strangers for help and she had been quite surprised when Akihito had done so at the coffee shop. That was one of the differences between men and women she had often noticed; Akira was the same way when they drove anywhere together.

"Ah, I wonder if that's it," Akihito exclaimed, and Toko peered through the windshield. Sure enough, there was a large white building that could easily be a terraced house, set back some distance from the road.

"I'm pretty sure that that is it," Akihito said confidently, and parked the car.

When they stepped out, the wet, night air sent a chill through Toko's body, and she reached back inside the car for the cardigan.

"It looks like Mother was right," she said with a smile, and offered Akihito the larger sweater, but even though he was only wearing a short-sleeved shirt, he refused.

"That's all right, I'm used to it. I often have to go out in the night to check on my kiln." He put his arm around Toko's shoulders as if to protect her from the cold wind.

They walked up to the building and started to check the names of the occupants. There were six houses in all, but the first five listed no Terauchis. When they came to the sixth nameplate, they both gave a small exclamation of satisfaction.

Terauchi, Shohei/Reika.

Toko felt her pulse race, but noticed Akihito looking around him as if he were disappointed.

"It doesn't look as though there's anyone home," he murmured.

"Maybe not, but why don't you ring the bell anyway?"

Akihito pressed the button on the side of the door and they heard a chime ring somewhere in the house, but nobody came to the door. Next he knocked loudly and called out Reika's name.

He had called out three times when the door of the next house opened and a woman in her forties looked out at them suspiciously. Living in a terraced house and sharing the same walls and roof, she must have been able to hear him calling.

"Excuse me, but are the Terauchis out today?" Akihito asked.

"Yes, you won't find anyone there at this time of night."

"What? Do you mean that they don't have any children?"

"Yes, that's right."

"Do you have any idea where the two of them might go at this time of night?"

The woman gave them a careful look for a moment, then slipped on some sandals and came over to where they were standing. She was nice looking and wore her hair pulled back in a ponytail. Toko guessed that she was probably about the same age as Reika.

"Excuse me," she asked, "but would you mind telling me what you want with them?"

"Oh, I *am* sorry. We're old friends of Reika Terauchi, and as we happened to be in the area, we thought we'd drop by and say hello."

"In that case, I suppose that you haven't heard that Mr. Terauchi is in the hospital?"

"No, what's the matter with him? Is he sick?"

"He had an accident on the expressway about six months ago. His car hit a truck and he's been hospitalized in Otsuki ever since."

"Oh, so Mrs. Terauchi has gone to see him in the hospital, has she?"

"No, she doesn't go every day—" The woman broke off in apparent confusion.

"Could you tell us where she is now?"

"I don't know if I should say this or not, but recently she's started to work part-time at a bar in Fuji-Yoshida. I suppose that things being the way they are, she doesn't have much money to spend, and it must be very difficult for her, sitting at home alone every night. She goes out in the early evening and the bar is especially busy at weekends, so I don't expect she'll be back for a long while yet."

"Working in a bar?"

They looked at each other in surprise.

"Excuse me, but the Terauchis first met at work, didn't they?" Toko asked. She realized that it was a rather strange question, but she felt that she had to know.

"Yes, that's right."

"Did they move here in 1981, as soon as they were married?"

"No, I heard Mr. Terauchi went to work in California for an American company for two years, so Reika gave up her job to accompany him. They moved here when they came back, since he was given a job in the laboratory here."

"He's the same age as Reika, isn't he?" Toko guessed.

The other woman looked at her in surprise. "No, he's six years younger than her, but they made such a good couple." She looked up at the darkened windows of the house and heaved a sigh.

"Do you know the name of the bar where Reika's working?" Akihito asked. He took out the map he had of the area and the woman pointed it out to him. It was called Mizu Basho and was situated a little outside the city center.

They thanked the woman for her help and walked back to the car in silence.

Toko felt the first shadow of doubt slip into her mind. This was not at all the way she had anticipated Reika Terauchi to be.

III

The car moved off again through the night, back the way it had just come. They passed the entrance to the expressway and then the vast Fujikyu Highlands amusement gardens on their left.

"We should be coming up to Fuji-Yoshida soon," Akihito muttered.

Toko, meanwhile, was habitually reviewing all she knew about Reika Terauchi.

Six years earlier, thirty-six-year-old Reika Asai had married thirty-year-old Shohei Terauchi, who was one of her colleagues at Toyo Oil. Shohei had gone to America to work for a company in California and she had given up her job in order to accompany him. She could very easily have known about this move before she married him, which would explain why Okito had said, "This person is going to go far away from me."

When the couple had come back from America two years later, Reika had gone to live by Lake Kawaguchi near her husband's new place of work. However, at the end of last year, he had been injured in a car accident and had been confined to a hospital bed ever since. She wondered what the woman next door had meant when she said, *It must be very difficult for her, sitting at home alone every night*, and why she talked about them having been *such a good couple*—in the past tense.

It was much more lively in the town center of Fuji-Yoshida than it had been by the lake. The rain, which stopped for a while, returned with renewed strength. The neon lights of the town seen through their water-splattered windshield looked like surrealistic webs of color.

Akihito gripped the steering wheel in silence as he searched for the bar, and he eventually found it without asking Toko's help.

They pulled into the parking lot, and peering out of the window, Toko saw the name of the bar written in a dim orange neon light that looked ready to go out at any moment.

"It's quite a long way from the town center, so I had a bit of trouble finding it, but if we had come straight here from her house, we could probably do it in about ten minutes, I should think," Akihito theorized.

He seemed to think that this was a reasonable distance for someone to travel for a part-time job.

They both stepped out of the car. The bar was very small and was crammed in between two old apartment buildings. It was still only about 8:30 in the evening, but the cold rain was enough to keep everyone off the streets and the area was as deserted as if it were midnight. However, the moment Akihito opened the door of the bar, Toko was forcefully reminded that this was Saturday night and that they were in a tourist area.

There was only a short bar and five tables, but the place was packed with couples and young people all drinking and talking loudly.

The whole place was decorated to resemble a mountain hut with the walls covered with pictures of wildflowers or the mountains and lakes of the area. The room was filled with cigarette smoke and it was rather dusty, so Toko, who was more used to the clean bars in the city, found it difficult to relax.

"Hello . . ."

Everyone called out a greeting as they walked in and sat down on a couple of empty stools by the door.

The bartender was a man in his midforties; he was being helped by two girls, but they were all very busy and it was some time before the girl who was standing nearest came over to them with some towels for them to wipe their hands on.

"What can I do for you?" she asked, and waited for their order. She had long hair and was wearing a red dress.

"A couple of whiskeys and water, please."

Toko looked at the woman carefully. She was wearing heavy eye shadow and eyeliner, which gave her a rather severe look, but when Toko looked closer, she realized that beneath the garish makeup, the woman had a gentle, roundish face with an attractive straight nose. She was wearing too much lipstick and it had been applied in a way that changed the shape of her mouth entirely. She was not as young as she had first appeared either, but her complexion was still good; she was probably in her late thirties—maybe even a little older.

The woman went to give the bartender their order, and suddenly it seemed to Toko that she could see through the mask of makeup to the beautiful, gentle face below.

"Reika . . ." she said before she realized what she was doing. "You are Reika Asai—sorry, Terauchi—aren't you?"

The other woman looked up at her sharply. "How do you know that?" she asked coldly after a momentary pause.

"I'm sorry, you see we called on you at your home at Lake Kawaguchi and your next-door neighbor told us that we'd be able to find you here."

"Oh?" The woman looked annoyed. "And what were you doing at my home?"

"We wondered if you could tell us something about Okito Shirafuji," Akihito interjected. He had dropped Okito's name on her without any warning, as they had agreed he would.

Reika looked at them questioningly, as if she had never heard the name before.

"I'm talking about the man who worked for the Ruco Corporation and was responsible for inventing the SuperMini and numerous other successful products. He taught at the university while you were studying there, and I am sure that you must have known him. After that . . ."

"Okay . . . okay, I know who you mean now," Reika interrupted with an irritated smile. "He died recently, didn't he? I seem to remember hearing his name in the papers and on the television."

"Is that all? Don't you have any other, more personal memories of him?" Toko asked probingly. "I remember meeting you walking with him in Ginza in October of 1981, shortly before you were married. Don't you remember that at all?"

Reika looked at her blankly so Toko ran through the events of that evening in detail.

"I will never forget that evening, and I am sure that uncle must have written to you afterward and maybe even met you sometimes. Didn't he contact you before he died and maybe tell you—"

Suddenly Reika burst out with laughter. She tilted back her head and laughed so loudly that several of the other customers turned to see what the noise was about. Toko realized that she must be a little drunk.

"Don't be ridiculous. I don't know what you can be thinking of—" She broke out into laughter again and could not speak for a moment. "I remember that night now. It was the first time I had seen him in fourteen or fifteen years, since I graduated from university and I bumped into him in Ginza about an hour before we met you. Of course I had seen his pictures in the papers and magazines, so I recognized him immediately and said hello. He asked me what I was doing and I told him that I was about to get married and go to the States. He seemed very amused at meeting me in Ginza at that time of day and offered to buy me a coffee.

"We came out of the tea room, and next, who should we bump into but you? You know the rest; he got more and more drunk and then he came out with all that romantic rubbish. I was still very young and impressionable in those days and was about to leave the country shortly, so I found myself very moved and cried a little, but that was all there was to it."

"But . . . is that really true?"

"Of course it's true. Are you suggesting that I'm lying?"

"No, I'm sorry. . . ."

Toko realized now why the only picture she had found of Reika in Okito's album was one of her in a group of students. She felt very embarrassed.

The bartender poured their drinks and passed them to Reika, who put them on the bar in front of them, her purple nail polish catching the light as she did so.

"Just to be quite clear about this, you're saying that you

never met Okito Shirafuji again after 1981?'' Akihito said in a stern tone.

"Of course."

"And he never wrote or called you?"

"Never."

"So how did you feel when you read about his death in the newspapers?"

"I didn't really think about it at all. After all, he only taught me at college for a short time, and after that I never saw him again. We were complete strangers."

"Yes, I suppose you were."

Toko was deeply disappointed. "I had hoped that you might be able to tell us something about Uncle Okito that we didn't know. . . ."

Reika shot her an angry look. "Now let's get one thing straight. I don't know what you want from me, but I'm a happily married woman and I can do without people spreading rumors about me."

She put a cigarette in her mouth and lit it, then turning to one side, she blew out the smoke angrily.

Toko thought about the kind of life Reika must have been living with her husband confined to a hospital bed for the last six months and found that she couldn't meet her eyes any longer.

"How long have you been working here?" Akihito asked calmly.

"Only about three months so far."

"Every night?"

"Except Sundays."

"So that means that you were on the night of April twenty-eighth, right?"

"April twenty-eighth?" Reika lifted her eyebrows questioningly.

"Yes, the day before the Emperor's birthday. It was a Tuesday."

"Why do you want . . . But wait a minute, I remember now. That day was the first anniversary of this bar, and so the owner, some of the customers, and I went for a drive to

Hakone after we closed at twelve o'clock. There were six of us altogether and we ended up spending the night in a small hotel there. But just a minute, why do you want to know about that day in particular?''

The two of them went back to the car and sat there without turning on the lights. Akihito put a cigarette in his mouth, but then thought better of it and put it away again. The rain was coming down harder than ever and beat noisily on the roof.

"Do you know why I asked her about April twenty-eighth?" he asked eventually, but Toko did not answer. "That was the night that Yaeko went to the wedding at Atami and thought that someone had broken into her bedroom during her absence."

The police had told her about this, so Toko immediately understood what he was talking about.

"It occurred to me that it was possible for her to have broken into the house, stolen the black pearl ring, filled it with some lysin that she had gotten from her husband's laboratory, and then put it back before anyone realized it had been missing. She could have done that if she wanted revenge for my father's death, and that's why I asked her about her alibi.

"However, it looks like we were wrong. She has an airtight alibi, and while I'm not saying that we necessarily have to take her word for it, I think it's very unlikely that she was lying.''

"Why would she want revenge for your father's death?" Toko asked. "She could hardly even remember him. Poor Uncle Okito.''

"You shouldn't say that; after all, they only met each other once by accident and had a few drinks together in a Ginza nightclub.''

"You're right, I was such a fool to have believed what he said and to have made up that fairy-tale story about their eternal love, but all the same, I think it's a pity that he didn't have somebody like that whom he really loved. If he did, he would have been much happier; that's why I said 'poor Uncle.' ''

Toko began sobbing uncontrollably, and as she did so, she found that she could still picture the beautiful, gentle Reika she had met in Ginza that night in her mind's eye. It occurred to her that she had probably loved Okito since she was a child and had felt jealous of the older woman ever since they met. She had been jealous of her, but had also wanted to be like her. She wanted to experience a love that would stand the test of time and to have her heart bound to someone else's for eternity.

"I was stupid," she said vehemently. "I should never have come here. If I hadn't, I'd still have been able to believe that despite the lonely way he died, Uncle Okito wasn't alone. I could have continued to believe the stupid story I dreamed up about them."

Akihito put his hands on her shaking shoulders and drew her to him, then brushing the tears from her cheeks, he turned her face toward his.

"I think that my father was happy to the end," he said. "Whatever people may say about him, he was able to devote his whole life to his work, and I think that wherever he is now, he must be very happy; after all, it was through him that we were able to find each other like this."

His lips wiped the last of her tears from her cheek and then found hers. Toko's body still shook slightly, but her mind went blank and her body seemed to melt into his.

6
Tragedy—Again

THE POSSIBILITY OF A CONNECTION BETWEEN THE LYSIN
that was found at Okito Shirafuji's house and Ryuta's airplane
crash was being taken seriously by the authorities.

Before the search of Okita's home, the crash of Ryuta's
Beechcraft had been treated purely as an accident and Yaeko's murder as the work of someone who held a personal
grudge against her, but suddenly, a new theory started to
gain acceptance, namely, that both deaths had been engi-
neered by Okito Shirafuji while he was still alive.

Both the methods used and the timing involved made this
theory credible. The last time that Ryuta used the Beechcraft
had been March 14, which was ten days before Okito's death,
so it was, indeed, feasible that Okito had tampered with it
after that date. All he needed to do was to slip into the airfield
at night when nobody was about, drain off a cupful of fuel
from the main tank of the plane, and replace it with an equal

amount of water. The plane was parked in the open, and such an act would not be difficult to pull off.

The same was true in Yaeko's case. She and Okito had once been lovers and he could easily have thought up some excuse to visit her or even become involved with her again. In either case, all he had to do was steal the black pearl ring, hide the lysin behind the pearl, fashion a small barb that would scratch her finger, and then slip the ring back before she realized that it was gone.

There was circumstantial evidence to back up this theory. A fountain pen inscribed with Okito's name had been found under Yaeko's bed, and although there was no telling when it got there, the carpet in the room had been relaid at the end of February and the housekeeper swore that the pen had not been there then. It would have been quite possible, however, for Okito to have visited the house sometime between the end of February and his death on March 24.

If Okito was guilty of these two murders, then the obvious motive was revenge. Nevertheless, as some of the people involved with the investigation pointed out, he had chosen very uncertain means of going about it. Why, it was asked, didn't he just kill them directly while he was still alive? Wakao was convinced that he was right, though, and defended his theory eloquently.

"As we all know, Okito Shirafuji was a genius in the true sense of the word, and I think it's likely that he was a very proud man. If he had killed Yaeko and Ryuta while he was still alive, he'd have been one of our first suspects, and if he was arrested, everyone would hear about it. Even if we failed to prove anything, people would say that he was not man enough to cope with his rejection at the company and they'd scorn him for his small-mindedness.

"He'd have found such words insupportable. Why, he didn't even want people to think he had committed suicide, so he chose a method that would make it look as if he died naturally. But before he did so he made preparations for his revenge.

"I will admit that there was a certain amount of luck involved in his plans coming to fruition, but he probably felt that the odds were on his side. If he didn't succeed one hundred percent, he'd still have given his intended victims an awful shock and also have reminded people of the terrible way he was treated by the company. In fact, his failure might well have been more effective than success: not only would he win the sympathy of the people, but he'd also be able to punish the executives of Ruco for their callousness.

"Finally, the fact that he was already dead at the time of both murders guaranteed that we would never be able to prove for certain whether he was responsible or not, or prosecute him for his crimes. I think this is the kind of plan that only a genius like Okito could conjure up and that it was one that he would have thought was worth betting his life on."

Whether Okito was responsible or not, the Ogikubo police had to concentrate on solving Yaeko Ichihara's murder; Ryuta's plane crash fell under the jurisdiction of the Five Lakes police station and it was up to them to work with the crash investigation committee to determine whether the cause was natural or not.

If they were to decide that Okito was responsible for Yaeko's death, the first things they had to discover were his source for the lysin and the method he'd found to surreptitiously put it into her ring. Until they were able to trace the lysin, there was no way for them to lay the blame for the murder on him. He was said to have friends in all fields of science and they had to check all of these out as possible sources for the chemical.

His role in the murder remained unclear, though, for someone else with a private grudge against Yaeko could just as easily have killed her. In that case the lysin could have been planted in his house in an effort to frame Okito. Thus the police had to check on everyone who had a possible motive for killing Yaeko or who would benefit from her death.

At the same time as they were proceeding with these two lines of investigation, the police had one more very important task to deal with: to ensure that there would be no more victims.

If one accepted the theory that Okito was the murderer, there was no reason why he should stop at Ryuta and Yaeko; why not a third or fourth victim as well?

One thing on which they were all agreed was that if there was going to be a third victim, Koji was the likeliest candidate. He was three years younger than Ryuta—fifty-two now—and when the company was first formed in 1967, he left the bank where he had been employed until then to become vice-president. He had been put in charge of the company's accounts, but everyone agreed that he lacked his elder brother's charisma. Ryuta was very forceful, a man of action, while Koji was more nervous and conservative, although it could be said that he was the more reliable of the two. He tended to leave the general running of the company to Ryuta, but it was rumored that when it came to Okito, he was the most critical of them all.

When questioned, his cousin Hiroshi Chino, had said, "He had always been in charge of the accounts and I think that was why he behaved the way he did when he saw the vast amounts of money that Okito was using on his research."

However, after Okito died, Yaeko had had a slightly different story. "Both his brothers were recognized as geniuses at what they did, and he found himself sandwiched between them ever since he was a young boy. On top of that, Ryuta had always tended to favor the youngest of the three, Okito, and so Koji had grown up with something of an antipathy toward his younger brother."

After a great deal of discussion at the Ogikubo station and central HQ, the police decided to ask their colleagues in Kitazawa, who covered the area in which Koji lived, if they could step up the patrols in the vicinity of his house; at the same time, Ruco hired some bodyguards to keep a constant eye on him.

He had his car checked to make sure that it had not been tampered with and his wife, Harue, checked his suits, tiepins, cuff links, and even his shoes in order to make sure that no lysin had been planted there.

On May 28, an executive meeting took place at the Ruco head office, and as expected, it was announced that Koji would become the next president of the company. Hiroshi Chino was promoted to executive director and a stockholders' meeting was called for the following month to nominate two new executives.

Ruco had always been very much of a family company, with Ryuta, Koji, Okito, and Hiroshi holding eighty percent of the total stock. Ryuta had thirty percent, Koji and Okito twenty percent each, and Hiroshi ten percent, although Okito had returned his shares to the company two years earlier to act as security for the loan he took for research funds. After his death, Yaeko managed to acquire some of his stock, but most of it went to Ryuta. When Ryuta died, all of his shares went to his wife, Hisako, but she had no interest in the running of the company and signed over her voting rights to Koji.

After Koji's promotion to president of the company, security arrangements were increased dramatically. He had always been a rather timid man and this facet of his personality now came to the fore. He had his car take a different route to the office every day, he never traveled far or went to play golf, and he refused to touch any of the presents he received from other companies. Even more, he refused to eat anything at the office except a packed lunch prepared by his wife and would only go to three restaurants that he had frequented for a long time.

"I think he's taking it a bit too far," Toko's mother remarked one evening as the two of them were eating their dinner together. "Assuming Okito planned something while he was still alive, the possibilities are rather limited. He is certainly in no condition to attack Koji's car or poison his food in a restaurant."

"But if he had an accomplice . . ." Toko began.

"If that's so, then he'd have used his accomplice to kill Yaeko, and if Ryuta's accident was planned, he'd have used

his accomplice again. Why would he choose to use such a
hit-or-miss method? Then again, if someone else is killing
them, someone who wants to put the blame on Okito, he still
wouldn't attack Koji's car. That would rather give the game
away, don't you think?''

Toko looked at her mother in amazement. Sachiko was
always such an easygoing person that such sharp observations
from her seemed incredible.

"Yes . . . but you don't think anything's going to happen
to Father, do you?'' she asked.

This caught Sachiko off guard and her expression froze for
a moment. "Of course he'll be all right. Don't worry, he's
done nothing to hurt Okito, and anyway, I'm here to keep an
eye on him.'' She spoke in a jovial tone to stop Toko from
worrying.

*Assuming Okito planned something while he was still
alive* . . . Sachiko's words repeated themselves in Toko's
mind and they awoke the memory of her dream. Once again,
she could hear Okito's voice saying *I will send them all death
from here on top of the clouds.*

A shudder ran through her and she suddenly felt that something terrible would happen again.

Her premonition came true a mere ten days later.

II

As far as the Ruco Corporation was concerned June 10
was an even more important day than the company's foundation day in October, for on that day in 1974, Okito's Super-
Mini had appeared on the market. Such was its success and
popularity that the Ruco brand became famous not only in
Japan but throughout the world. They had needed this coup
to launch them as a major company, and the following year
they completed a new factory at Yokosuka; the year after
that, they opened their fifteen-story office-building headquarters in the Marunouchi district of Tokyo. Both buildings
were opened on June 10, and although Ryuta was in no way
a superstitious man, he considered June 10 a consecrated day

for the firm. Every year, a ceremony was held at head office and the president addressed the company employees.

This year marked the twentieth anniversary of the company's founding, and its directors had originally planned a special celebration to commemorate this fact, but due to the recent spate of deaths, they decided to opt instead for a more modest ceremony. At the same time, however, the executives were eager to use the event as an opportunity to dispel the prevailing mood of disaster that had gripped the company since Ryuta's death.

Despite the fact that it fell in the rainy season, June 10 dawned bright and clear. At ten o'clock in the morning, the five hundred staff members of the head office all gathered in the hall on the seventh floor. It was a bit of a squeeze to fit them all in as the hall was not very large; despite serving as the site of the company's ceremonies and the occasional party, it was no more than a large conference room, plain in decor, with just a small wooden dais at one end to set it apart from the other rooms in the building. If anything, such plainness underscored the youth of the company.

A table had been set in the middle of the dais and a bouquet of flowers placed on the left. Light flooded in through the south and west windows, which overlooked the Emperor's palace, and helped get the ceremony off to a bright start. As always, it began at ten o'clock in the morning, with the president—now Koji Shirafuji—mounting the stage. Silence immediately descended on the room.

Koji was not a particularly small man, but he could not compare to his brother, who always seemed twice as large as life. He was wearing a morning coat and walked slowly across the stage with his shoulders back. A small television camera at the foot of the stage followed his progress across the stage, transmitting the whole ceremony to the other offices and factories across the country.

"Until a month ago, I had never dreamed that it would be I who addressed you all on this happy day," Koji began. His gray hair was neatly brushed back and he smiled brightly, hoping to inject a note of happiness into the proceedings, but he was feeling so tense that the smile froze on his lips almost immediately.

"I am sure that you don't need me to tell you that my brother, the last president of this company, died on the twelfth of May, and that on the twenty-eighth I was chosen to take his place. For this reason, I will take the opportunity of this happy day to address you all for the first time in my capacity as president."

He gripped the table before him and looked around the audience in front of him. He had always liked public speaking, and as he continued, his tenseness dissipated and he was able to continue in his normal fashion.

"The last three months have brought with them a tragedy that nobody at Ruco could ever have foreseen, and in fifty days, we lost three of our best executives. It is not surprising that you are all feeling very shocked and worried about the future of the company, but you must remember that it is our performance during this trying period which will shape the future of the company. For this reason I want to call on each and every one of you to do all that you possibly can to ensure that the future will be as bright, if not brighter, than our past already has been."

He took a deep breath and raised his voice. "While we will never be able to replace the three people that have been taken from our midst, that is all in the past now. We must not allow ourselves to become preoccupied with the past, we must only think of the future. I am not afraid of what the future might bring and I—"

At that moment the desk in front of him exploded with a thunderous roar. The room was filled with flames and fragments of wood, and Koji's body was thrown into the air in a cloud of smoke. It flew in a strangely graceful curve to land headfirst at the back of the stage.

III

The sound of sirens filled the morning air in the Marunouchi district as police cars, fire engines, and ambulances
roared past, all headed in the same direction.

They raced down Hibiya Road, and the other cars all pulled
over to make way for them. The pedestrians all stopped in
their tracks and looked back in the direction from which they
had heard the sound of an explosion a few minutes earlier.

I wonder if all this fuss has something to do with that noise
I heard just now, each pedestrian thought. Come to think of
it, that's the direction of the Ruco Corporation. I wonder if
something has happened there again?

The businessmen in the area looked on, their faces showing the mixture of fear and curiosity they all felt. In the vicinity of the Ruco building itself, people rushed out into the
street or clustered around the windows, their eyes fixed on
the wisp of white smoke that filtered through the open windows on the seventh floor.

As the police cars and fire trucks arrived on the scene,
they pulled up in front of the building and their occupants
disappeared inside, but by the time the firemen showed up,
the small fire caused by the explosion had already been ex-
tinguished and only a trace of white smoke was left in the
air. Flames from the explosion had reached the folding screen
at the back of the stage and set it afire, but this small confla-
gration was soon dealt with by the people on hand at the
time.

Koji was lying in the flowers that had stood to the left of
the stage and his clothes showed some burn marks and were
ripped open around his stomach. He had lost a lot of blood,
and although their efforts seemed hopeless, the paramedics
rushed to put him on a stretcher and do what they could for
him.

Koji was the only victim of the explosion, and as soon as
he had been carried away and the remaining flames extin-
guished the police were able to start their investigations.

The investigation fell under the jurisdiction of the Special

Squad from central HQ and Inspector Hijikata was put in charge of it. The Special Squad was a team of investigators that was formed to deal with kidnappings, air crashes, explosions, and computer crime, its members having specialized knowledge in all these fields. Hijikata was generally accepted as their authority on explosives.

The team consisted of ten officers, who started by carefully gathering all the fragments of wood and metal scattered around the room by the explosion. Few members of the audience had dared to approach the stage after the blast, so it remained more or less untouched.

Other officers from the local station rounded up the employees who had been gathered in the hall at the time, and, separating them into groups, they questioned each of them. The newly promoted Hiroshi Chino and the administrative director, Sakai, remained in the hall to answer the questions put to them by Inspector Hijikata. Hijikata was a man in his midforties, rather short, but very powerfully built and rather good-looking.

"So," he was saying, "two or three minutes after the president mounted the stage, the table in front of him exploded and he was thrown backward, is that correct?" he asked, to verify what Hiroshi had told him.

"Yes, that's right," Hiroshi replied.

"And where were you at the time?"

"Over there in the front row to the left of the stage." Hiroshi pointed to a row of seats.

"I was on the very left and Chino was sitting next to me," Sakai put in. "I was acting as the master of ceremonies, so I had to go up on stage several times during the ceremony."

"I see, you were lucky to escape uninjured."

Hiroshi's face convulsed involuntarily; he had been so overwhelmed by the immensity of the disaster that he had not thought about the danger to himself.

"Can you tell me exactly what time the explosion took place?" Hijikata continued.

"Sakai opened the ceremony at exactly ten o'clock and then handed the stage over to the president almost immediately, so I think it must have been three or four minutes past ten.''

"Yes, I think that's about right," Sakai put in.

"I see . . ." said the detective, and then proceeded to have them describe in as much detail as possible how loud the explosion had seemed to them and how the flames had appeared.

"Was the bomb planted in the table then?" Sakai asked.

"I think so."

"Was it a time bomb?"

"Probably. By the way, is the door to this room usually kept locked?" Hijikata asked, slightly changing the direction of his inquiry.

"Yes, there are two doors and both are kept locked all the time," Sakai answered. "The keys are kept in the security office on the first floor by the rear exit and anyone who wants to use it has to go there and sign one out."

"This room is not only used for ceremonies like this," Hiroshi interjected. "Whenever we have a large meeting, we use this room."

"Can you find out who was the last person to use it?" Hijikata asked.

"Yes, we can ask the guard to look in his notebook."

"Well, you can do that for me later. Next I want you to tell me a bit about this building; how many entrances are there?"

"Two," Hiroshi replied. "The main entrance and the rear one, although there's an emergency exit at the end of the corridor on each floor that leads out to the fire escape."

"Is the emergency exit usually kept locked?"

"Yes, from the inside. In an emergency, the door can be unlocked and used to escape."

"And it cannot be opened from outside?"

"That's right."

"How about the main entrance? Do you keep a check on people coming in that way?"

"There are two receptionists and a guard on duty there. The staff all have badges, although they are all known by sight and so obviously they can freely pass in or out. Visitors have to report to reception and say what their business is. If anyone suspicious comes, the guard is there to question them.''

''So that means that nobody but staff members or official visitors is able to pass through the main entrance,'' the detective summarized.

''Yes.''

''And what about the rear entrance?''

''There's a guard on duty there, too, and although several people come to deliver things to the canteen or to clean the building, they're all supposed to present their identification before they're allowed to enter.''

''So that means that a check is kept there as well then.''

''Yes, although I don't know how strictly the rules are actually observed,'' Hiroshi admitted with a sick smile. ''Especially when it comes to the rear entrance; I think it would be quite easy for someone to slip in while a delivery was being made.''

''But either way, if the crime was committed by someone outside the company, they would have two obstacles to pass, first to get into the building and second to get their hands on the key to this room.''

''Yes, and the second one should be very difficult for them to do. The guard would be sure to check to see who he was giving the key to, and it would be impossible for them to get it without his knowing.''

''Yes, and anyway, someone from outside the company wouldn't have any way of knowing which of the keys opened the door to this particular room,'' Sakai added.

''Mmm . . .'' Hijikata nodded slowly and walked away. He checked on the progress of his men who were collecting the evidence and photographing the scene and then came back to Hiroshi and Sakai.

''Just so I can get it straight in my mind, I'd like to see how this room is locked up.''

He started by walking over to the windows, and Hiroshi and Sakai obediently followed. The room faced southwest

and several of the windows were wide open. It was too early
yet for the air-conditioning to be turned on, so several windows had been opened before the ceremony began in order
to let some air into the room; the remainder had been opened
after the explosion in an attempt to get rid of the smoke.
Since the room was on the seventh floor, it was very unlikely
that anyone could have gotten in that way, and there were no
marks on the outside of the building to show that any such
attempt had been made. Outside, the sun shone peacefully
on the trees of the palace complex as if nothing had happened.

Next, Hijikata walked toward the corridor. Here the wall
was lined with smoked-glass windows about three feet high,
with long, rectangular, revolving windows on top, which
could be opened for ventilation purposes.

All the bottom windows were shut and locked, but Hijikata walked along the wall checking each one of them. He
had gone about twenty feet from the door when he suddenly
stopped. One of the top windows, which were about two and
a half feet wide by one foot high was open a couple of inches.

"Was this opened this morning?" he asked sharply.

"I'm afraid I don't know," Hiroshi answered, "but it's
possible that it has been left like that for some time."

They hurriedly checked the rest of the windows and found
that the bottom windows were firmly fastened, but three of
the top ones had been left open a fraction.

"I'll check with the janitors and staff, but I think these
may have been left open for some time. Somebody probably
opened them to let some air into the room and then forgot to
close them again when they left the room," Sakai said in
consternation. "The guards will have checked the outside
windows carefully, but probably nobody ever thought of
looking at these narrow little windows facing the corridor,
especially as they are set so high up."

"Yes, they may be small, but there's plenty of room for a
man to slip through them into the room," Hijikata said with
frown. "If they were opened fully, it would be no trick to
get into the room through them. That removes one obstacle

from the murderer's path; he only had to get into the building without attracting attention and he could have gotten into this room with no trouble.''

IV

Koji Shirafuji died in the hospital without ever regaining consciousness. The cause of his death was listed as internal injuries caused by the explosion.

The news was received at the Ruco Corporation at 11:00 A.M., and at 12:30 an investigation headquarters was set up at the Marunouchi police station. Here, at one o'clock, a meeting was held to discuss the case.

The investigation was headed by a detective sergeant from HQ, with the chief of the investigation section at HQ and the Marunouchi station chief as his assistants. The two officers from HQ had to sit in on all the investigations currently under way in the Tokyo metropolitan area, so they could not always be present at meetings like this, but this case was judged to be so important that everyone involved managed to attend.

"We're still investigating the scene of the explosion, but I'll fill you in on the facts as far as we know them at the moment," Hijikata said. "With regard to the bomb itself, we've been able to find fragments of a battery and a timing device, but everything else was destroyed in the explosion. From what we can tell, it would appear that the explosive was in a malleable form and was wrapped around the battery, timer, and fuse before being hidden in the desk on the stage.''

Everyone in the room listened intently.

"Judging from the size of the explosion, we think that there was probably no more than about four ounces of explosive used and that it was planted at the closest point to the victim—that is to say, under the desktop and above the drawer. This would mean that even if the drawer had been opened, the bomb would remain hidden, but when it exploded, it would be close to the victim's stomach and would therefore be in a position to cause the worst possible injuries. In fact, it's quite possible that the bomb was purposely made so small and fitted where it was in order that it would kill the intended victim, but not injure anyone else in the room.''

"First the president, then the managing director, now the new president . . .'' someone among his audience was heard to mutter.

"Next,'' the officer in charge called out, ignoring the mutterings, "I would like to call on Superintendent Shikada to report on how the bomb could have been planted in the building.''

Shikada had been in charge of questioning the employees in the building and had also received a report from Hijikata on the results of his search of the room.

"First, with regard to the time of entry into the building,'' he began, "I think it was probably done during the day. At night, the guards check the whole building to ensure that nobody's left in there and that all the doors and windows are locked, then they switch over to a computerized alarm system, so I think that it was impossible for anyone to break in at that time. During the daytime, however, someone could enter through the main entrance without much trouble, on the pretext of seeing someone in the company, or they could slip in through the rear exit during a delivery.

"Once inside the building, getting inside the room is easy. There's a row of windows two and a half feet wide by one foot three inches high separating the room from the corridor, and three of these were left open slightly. The room was last used on Monday, June 1, for a meeting of the sales staff. When I questioned the people who attended, half of them seemed to remember the windows having been open at that time, but nobody could be sure how long they had been left like that.

"The room itself is situated around a bend in the corridor and is out of sight of the rest of the floor, so it would be easy for somebody who knew this, to slip in through one of the windows, plant the bomb, and get away again without being seen.''

This was all the information the police had been able to

gather at this time, so the officer in charge asked if there were any questions.

"We have just heard that the bomber could have slipped in through the window and planted his bomb, but how much time would this require?" one of the veteran detectives asked.

"I would say, in a case like this, anywhere between five and ten minutes," Hijikata replied.

At this, a collective gasp was heard in the room; nobody had imagined that it could be done so quickly.

"What type of explosive was used in the device?" another detective wanted to know.

"We haven't had a chance to analyze it yet, but I think it's safe to say that it was nitroglycerine," Hijikata replied. "For those of you who do not know, nitroglycerine is a colorless, oil-based explosive. It's made by mixing glycerine, nitric acid, and sulfuric acid, and can be produced quite easily by anyone with a grounding in chemistry."

"Is it difficult to get the ingredients?"

"No, none of them are very rare. Glycerine is used for numerous purposes, aside from medicine, for example, as a lubricant and in the production of makeup and soap. All are very easy to buy and can be obtained from drugstores, fertilizer retailers, or paint shops."

"How about the timer?"

"There's nothing difficult about that, and they're quite readily available. There are also lots of books available on the black market that describe how to construct bombs of this nature."

"So you mean that anyone could have done it?" one of the younger detectives murmured, and Hijikata turned in his direction.

"Yes, that's exactly what I mean. Although I think we must assume that they had a basic knowledge of explosives and timing devices. However, everything the perpetrator needed can be purchased quite easily; although this is quite regrettable, we mustn't forget it."

The room fell silent as the detectives realized how difficult this case was becoming.

"With regard to the timing device," the investigation chief asked in order to break the silence. "Do you have any idea when it was set?"

"No, I'm afraid not," Hijikata answered. "If we'd been able to find it before the explosion, we might've had a chance, but now it's been completely destroyed and we only have a few fragments left to go on."

"But can't you make a guess?"

Hijikata shook his head. "If they used two clocks, one that registered days and another hours, they could set it so it went off at a particular time on any particular day. It could have been set at any time."

"Even seventy days ago?"

"Yes, quite easily."

"When you say seventy days, are you referring to some time before March 24, when Okito Shirafuji died?" the station chief asked, and the head of investigation squad nodded in silence.

"Mmm . . . I see," The Marunouchi station chief said. "According to the staff at the office, this ceremony has been held on the tenth of June every year for the last ten years, and it always opens at ten o'clock with a speech by the president, so it would have been quite possible for someone to think of that seventy days or more ago and set the bomb."

"Yes, and it was done in such a way that it wouldn't hurt any of the other staff, just the president, Koji Shirafuji," the investigation chief said.

Could it really be the work of a dead man? everyone wondered.

Nobody could doubt the possibility any longer. It was as if a dark cloud hung over them all and nobody was able to escape from its gloom.

7

The Pursuit

I

THIS TIME THE POLICE WASTED NO TIME JUMPING INTO AC-
tion. On the same day that Koji was killed by the explosion
at Ruco's head office, several men from the investigation
squad turned up at Hiroshi Chino's house in Meguro and
started a thorough search of the whole building. They were
determined to prevent any further crimes from being committed, and the odds on Hiroshi being the fourth target were
very high.

The fifty-year-old cousin of the Shirafuji brothers on his
mother's side, Hiroshi had graduated from the university with
a degree in engineering and gone to work for an electronics
company. He joined the Ruco Corporation in 1970, three
years after its inception and was soon given an executive
post, in accordance with Ryuta's policy of hiring family
members as much as possible. He was a gentle man and had
often complained to Ryuta and Koji about their treatment of
Okito, which made it unlikely that Okito would want to kill

128

him. However, there was no guessing Okito's state of mind toward the end of his life; he may well have decided to avenge himself on all the executives of the company, regardless of their individual behavior toward him.

If this was so, Hiroshi was next in line. After Ryuta's death he had been promoted to the post of executive director, and with Koji's death he was the most likely candidate for the post of president.

The police were strongly inclined by this point to the belief that Okito had committed the murders, and so when they came to the Chino house, they checked to see if there was a bomb hidden anywhere, if anything edible had been laced with lysin, or if there was any other trap that could have been set sometime in the past.

The Chinos lived in a well-situated six-room, two-story house, half-Japanese and half-Western in style. Hiroshi was still tied up at the office while the search got under way, but Sachiko and Toko were on hand, and both wife and daughter watched the proceedings with worried looks on their faces. The search started at 5:00 P.M. and lasted for three hours.

Finally, the officer in charge entered the kitchen and walked over to where Toko and Sachiko were sitting. "We've gone over the house from top to bottom," he announced. "We've even looked under the floorboards, and I'm able to assure you that there were no explosives to be found anywhere."

"That's a relief," Sachiko said with a sigh.

"We haven't managed to find anything else that looked like a trap, and all that remains now is lysin. As you know, Yaeko Ichihara was poisoned by lysin hidden in her ring, but I understand that your husband does not wear any rings or other jewelry close to his body, correct?"

"Yes, only his watch."

"The officers at the office have already checked that, but they couldn't find anything." Hiroshi had three other watches in the house and these had also tested safe. "Therefore, I think that in your husband's case, it's more likely that the poison could be administered orally."

"Orally?"

"Yes, although it's much more effective if it enters the body directly, lysin is equally fatal if ingested orally, and since it's easier to administer a large dose that way, it's probably a more reliable way of killing somebody."

So saying, he produced two bottles, which he had found earlier on the shelf behind the table where Sachiko and Toko were sitting.

"Vitamin-C powder and Vitamin-E capsules. I understand that you and your husband take these twice a day; is that correct?"

"Yes, one capsule of Vitamin E and one teaspoonful of Vitamin C; I'm told they help fight fatigue and aging."

"Do you get them from a doctor?" the officer wanted to know.

"Yes, my brother-in-law is a doctor at a university hospital and he gets them for us. It's much cheaper that way, and anyway, they don't sell these in the drugstore."

The Vitamin-C bottle contained five hundred grams and the Vitamin-E bottle, five hundred capsules, so both bottles were quite large.

"How often do you buy them? About once every four months or so?"

"Yes, when I'm getting a bit short of one or the other, I just give my brother-in-law a ring and he brings them over when he's in the neighborhood."

"When was the last time?" The detective looked inside the bottles; the Vitamin-E one was still half-full, but the Vitamin-C one was almost empty.

"Around the middle of February, I had him bring me one of each, but I dropped the bottle of Vitamin E and it smashed to pieces, so I threw away the contents and had him bring me another. When was that now . . . ? Around the middle of March, I think."

"So that means you've had both of them since before Okito Shirafuji died, right?"

"Yes, I suppose so."

"Is there anything else like this that your husband takes?"

"Nothing that he eats, but he uses hair tonic and after-shave lotion every morning, doesn't he?" Sachiko turned to Toko. "What if he were to cut himself shaving and then put some poisoned after-shave on his face?"

"Now that you mention it, there are the bath salts, too," Toko remembered.

"We always use bath salts when we take a bath; what if he were to accidentally drink of mouthful of water, would it be dangerous?" Sachiko asked in horror.

The detective showed the trace of a smile but soon became serious again; he could not afford to leave anything to chance and would have it all checked.

"While we're on the subject, could you give me your brother-in-law's name and address, please? In case we need to get in touch with him."

He jotted the information down in his notebook, and then rounding up everything they were going to have checked, he took his leave.

"It's frightening, isn't it?" Toko said, after the officer was gone, her face ashen.

Strangely enough, Sachiko did not seem very alarmed. "There's nothing to worry about, your father has done nothing that would make Okito want to kill him."

"But the police and everybody seem to think that Okito did all this in order to destroy the company," Toko persisted.

"Very well then, but looking at all the murders to date, Okito only hurt the person he meant to hurt; he made quite sure not to hurt any outsiders. Besides, if he were to have put poison in our vitamin pills, there'd be a fifty-percent chance that I'd be the one to take the poison, not your father, and that would go against his policy."

"But what if there had been no other way?"

"No, Okito was a genius. If he really wanted to kill your father, he'd think of a way to do it without hurting anyone else. The police weren't able to find anything in the house and they're experts at what they do, so obviously Okito didn't want to hurt us."

Sachiko sounded so convinced that Toko finally allowed herself to relax.

The next day, however, something happened that proved her to have been quite wrong.

The front doorbell rang at 8:30 in the morning and Sachiko answered it to find two of the detectives from the previous day standing on the porch. Hiroshi had still not left for work, and even Toko, who usually slept late, had gotten up and was sitting in the kitchen.

"I'm sorry for disturbing you yesterday," one of the detectives said as he entered the house, "but I'm afraid that I have to inform you that lysin was discovered in the bottle of Vitamin E."

"What?" the three Chinos said, almost in unison.

"One of the capsules in the bottle was found to contain lysin. There was easily enough to be fatal if taken, but luckily it was still at the bottom of the bottle. Initially we guessed that whoever put it there must have done so in the hope that Mr. Chino would eventually take it and die, but . . ." He gave Hiroshi a piercing look. "Do you remember exactly when you bought that bottle of tablets?"

"No, I leave that kind of thing to my wife."

"I think it was the middle of March," Sachiko put in.

"That would mean that you bought it while Okito was still alive, wouldn't it?"

"Yes . . ."

"Well, I'm afraid that this wasn't the case."

They all looked at him in silence.

"Yesterday, the inspector asked you for your brother-in-law's name and address, and when we discovered the lysin, we got in touch with him directly. He was able to tell us exactly when he gave you the capsules. He said that he had dropped them off here for you on his way home from a funeral he had attended nearby."

"Now that you mention it, I seem to remember him saying something about a funeral," Sachiko murmured, but the detective ignored her.

"Well, it turns out that the funeral was on Saturday, March 28—four days after Okito died."

The two detectives looked over at Hiroshi.

"I'm very sorry, sir, but there are a few questions we'd like to ask you, and we wondered if you'd be so kind as to accompany us down to the station."

II

Toko sat at the same table at the back of the ivy-covered coffee bar and faced Akihito. It was four o'clock on Saturday, June 13, but despite the fact that it was a weekend, there were remarkably few customers.

"It's frightening," she said, without taking her eyes off the road outside, then remembered having said the same thing to her mother after the police had searched the house and taken away the bottom of vitamin pills. Thinking back on it now, she realized that it was not nearly so bad then as it was now. Things could hardly get any worse than they already were.

"So your father was summoned to the police station again today, was he?" Akihito asked with a worried frown.

"Yes, they've come for him at eight thirty every morning for the last three days."

"But surely they're still investigating the explosion; it doesn't necessarily mean that your father—"

"No," she interrupted. "Father says that their suspicions are now focused on him. They couldn't do anything about Uncle Okito now that he's dead and so they're putting all their energies into trying to prove that it was Father."

"And this is all because the poison was found in a bottle of pills that was delivered after my father's death, which means it couldn't have been his handiwork?"

When Akihito had called Toko that afternoon, she asked if she could see him right away. She had felt a cold coming on, so she had not gone to school the previous day; she had just been sitting around the house, not feeling like doing anything.

When he asked her where she wanted to meet him, she had suggested this coffee bar without a moment's hesitation, since she knew that here at least she would not run into any friends from college and would be able to sit and talk quietly to him without any interruptions. However, as soon as she saw him, she became very upset and cried slightly as she explained what had happened at her home since they had last met.

The press still had not learned that Hiroshi was the latest suspect, so the news came as a complete shock to Akihito. Toko was a little hysterical, and so he went over the story with her again, checking every detail.

"Yes, they were just beginning to believe that Uncle Okito was responsible for the deaths of Uncle Ryuta, Koji, and Yaeko when they came across the poisoned capsule at the bottom of the bottle. They realized that Okito could not very well have put it there after he died, and so suddenly they're thinking it was Father and that he tried to put the blame on Okito.''

"I suppose they think that he killed the other three in order to become president of the company?'' Akihito muttered.

"Yes, of course; he hasn't become the president yet, but with Ryuta and Koji out of the way, he's the most likely candidate.''

"Yes, I see. It can't be denied that he stands to benefit the most from the death of the other three,'' Akihito said candidly.

"Yes, and it would have been possible for him to have committed all the other murders. He could easily have drained some of the fuel from the fuel tank of the plane and replaced it with water to cause Uncle Ryuta's accident. The same goes for Yaeko. Being another managing director, he must have visited her house on numerous occasions in the past, and he only needed to know roughly where she kept things. He could easily have made up some excuse to go and visit her, then waited for the chance to steal her ring. He has a lot of friends from his university days who specialized in chemistry and any one of them could have supplied him with the lysin. He himself studied electronics, so a timer for the bomb would present no special problems, and he had free access to the room where it was planted at all times.''

"Yes," said Akihito, picking up her train of thought, "and he would have had plenty of opportunity to go to my father's house at Egota to steal one of his pens to leave beneath Yaeko's bed in order to throw the police off the scent. The same goes for the lysin; he's been to my father's house several times since the funeral, so it would have been simple for him to plant it in the closet next to my father's bedroom.''

"They say that he planted the poisoned capsule in the vitamin bottle to pretend that someone was trying to kill him, too.'' Toko bit her lip, trying to hold back the tears that again threatened.

"I see, and he put the poisoned capsule at the very bottom of the bottle so it would look as if it were mere luck that had saved him,'' Akihito said dispassionately. "Unfortunately, he made one fatal mistake. He didn't realize that the vitamins hadn't been delivered to the house until after my father had died, and that's what gave him away.

"But don't you think, Toko . . .'' He waited a short while until Toko had calmed down before going on. "The police are being a bit silly about it. If your father had really killed the other three and tried to put the blame on a dead man, he'd have been very careful about how he did every stage of it. If he was going to plant some poison in his own house to clear any doubt that might hang over him, he'd at least have checked to see when the vitamins were delivered to the house. This information was vital to the plan and he wouldn't have used the bottle without making quite sure first.''

"Yes, but it's not as simple as that. You see, Mother bought a bottle each of Vitamin C and E in February, but she dropped the bottle of E and smashed it. She ordered another bottle, but it didn't arrive until March 28, and Father didn't know anything about this. He thought that she'd gotten both of them in February.''

"Didn't your mother tell him that she'd bought a new bottle?''

"No, unfortunately, Mother can't remember having told him, and he told the police that she never mentioned it to him."

"I see." He remained deep in thought for a short while, then looked over at Toko again. "So the police think that he killed the other three and then tried to put the blame on my father, but made a slip. There is, however, another way of looking at it. What if someone killed the other three, someone who also meant to kill your father and put the blame for all four on my father. He wouldn't have known about your mother dropping the pills either and could have put the poison in by mistake."

"Yes . . . but that would mean that the murderer was still alive and wanted to kill my father." Toko suddenly felt frightened and a shudder ran down her spine. The next moment, however, an idea came to her. "There's still another explanation. . . ." She paused to gather her thoughts, but Akihito interrupted her.

"Oh yes, before I forget." He leaned forward slightly and moved his cold cup of coffee to one side. "About Reika Terauchi; I checked her alibi for April twenty-eighth and she was telling the truth. Apparently it really was the anniversary of the opening of the bar and she went to Hakone after closing time and spent the night in a hotel there. I telephoned the bar and talked to the landlord about it."

"April twenty-eighth? Oh, you mean the day that Yaeko thought someone had broken into her house?"

"Yes. Anyway, her alibi holds and there's no other way for her to have gotten her hands on the ring, so I suppose she can't have had anything to do with it."

Toko suddenly remembered Reika's heavily made-up face and purple nail polish. So she had nothing to do with Uncle Okito, after all, she thought sadly.

Now, when she thought back to that evening, she found that the shock of seeing her theory about Reika go up in smoke was nothing compared to the horror of subsequent events. She remembered how she had sat in Akihito's car in the parking lot with the lights out and how he had kissed her for the first time. She thought she'd been waiting for that moment since she first met him, but they had only met twice since then—once for a meal with Akihito's French artist friend and his wife to celebrate the end of the exhibition in Ginza, and once to see a show of the work of a famous American artist he liked.

He had not changed his attitude toward her since they kissed, but she felt that they were much closer than they had been before. She knew that they would continue to meet each other in this way until they reached the next stage in their relationship. She hated not being able to see him every day, but she knew that if she waited, their time would come. She could feel herself growing and was torn between fear and fascination to find herself standing at the threshold of adult romance.

"I must be very hard for you, your father being the suspect in a murder case," Akihito said in a soft voice, full of concern.

"But you were in the same situation until recently," she quickly replied.

"Yes, but I believed in his innocence. It's no use your worrying, you won't be able to do anything for him like that. The best thing you can is just trust him and wait; things are sure to sort themselves out eventually." He paused briefly and then exclaimed, "Oh, at times like this, I feel that I just want to go somewhere and forget about everything."

"I agree." Toko wanted to escape from the present more than anything.

"Really? Then why don't we do it?" Akihito said, looking at her.

Their eyes met and she felt herself drawn into his gaze. He had a well-shaped nose, his intelligent eyes were rather deep set under his thick eyebrows, his lips were well formed, and his chin was slightly pointed. His clothes were all from Paris and he wore his hair a little long. All these details combined to give him a rather Western look.

Uncle Okito . . . For a moment she saw Okito in his face, then a cold wave of sadness ran through her. How long would

Akihito remain beside her; would he, too, disappear one day?

She closed her eyes to drive these thoughts from her mind, and when she opened them again, she smiled back at him and said, "Yes, take me with you."

III

When Superintendent Ukyo Nakazato visited the old hotel on the southern shore of Lake Yamanaka, it was on a case completely unconnected to the Ruco murders.

It was Monday, June 15, and reports had come in that a burglar had emptied the safe of a hotel in Gotemba the night before and made off with a fortune in cash and bonds. The prefectural police had put out an alert and asked all the local stations to check for any suspicious figures or cars passing through their areas.

Although it was unusual for the station chief to become involved in a routine case like this, the area around the Five Lakes contained a large number of hotels and some of these put their guests' privacy before their duty to the police and thus were rather loath to reveal information. Nakazato had been stationed in the area for most of his career in the force and this, combined with his straightforward personality, tended to put him on friendly terms with most of the hoteliers. Thus he decided to visit two or three of the better hotels himself to see what he could learn.

That morning saw a break in the rainy season and Mount Fuji could be seen clearly, towering over the lake as he entered an old, wooden, northern European–style hotel. There was not a cloud in the sky and the sun shone brilliantly off the lake.

Nakazato had just about finished talking to the assistant manager and had decided that he would not be of any help when an old man with white hair and a walking stick ambled over.

"I heard that you were here and couldn't let you go without having a little chat first," the man announced.

"Oh, Mr. Azumayashiki, you look as fit as ever," Nakazato exclaimed.

"Thank you, although I daresay I am too fit by far for some people." He spoke with a smile and a sidelong glance at the assistant manager.

Mr. Azumayashiki was approaching ninety, but he was still the manager of the hotel. Of course he did not do very much real work now, but he was very popular among the guests and acted as a sort of figurehead. Nakazato was young enough to be his grandchild, but ever since he had solved the mystery of Yohei Wada's death at the villa in the Asahi Hills, they always stopped for a chat when they ran into each other.

The assistant manager, seeing that he would not be needed anymore, said good-bye and made his exit.

"It must be a month now since the plane carrying the president of the Ruco Corporation crashed into the lake there," Mr. Azumayashiki said, sitting down opposite Nakazato, his eyes on the sparkling surface of the lake. Of course the wreckage of the plane had been entirely cleared away by now and there was nothing to show that anything had happened.

"Yes, it happened on May 12, so it's a little over a month now."

"Do they know what caused it?"

"No, the crash investigation team has yet to issue its report, which is likely to take at least six months."

"Things have been very hard for Ruco ever since then, what with all these suspicious deaths," the old man said. "Talking of which, there was Okito Shirafuji's death, too, that was never properly explained either. I wonder if it really was just an accidental death like they say."

"Yes, they said all kinds of things in the press," Nakazato said.

"All the same, it's a terrible loss, he was such a genius. The Shirafuji family has often stayed at this hotel; they used to visit for long periods during the summer and New Year holidays, so I find it very difficult to think of them as strangers."

Nakazato was surprised. "You mean you knew Ryuta and Okito Shirafuji?"

"Yes, I used to know them very well indeed; I even used to play golf with Ryuta, but that was mostly during the early sixties when the company was still growing. After that, they tended to go abroad for their holidays, but Okito still came here. I suppose he felt a certain nostalgia about that period, because he continued to come here right up to the time of his death."

"Until his death? When was the last time you saw him?" The detective decided to pursue this unexpected lead.

"Let me see, that must have been March 17, it was a Tuesday, he came into the main dining room and drank a little wine with his meal."

"But that was only a week before he died." For some reason, Nakazato was very surprised to hear this. "Did he stay here that night?"

"No, he just had dinner and then went home. I usually went over to say hello to him, but I thought it would be more tactful of me to leave him alone that time, and now I regret having done so. I never guessed it would be the last time I saw him."

"What do you mean, 'tactful'?" Nakazato asked, keeping his eyes on the old man's face. "Do you mean that he wasn't alone?"

"That is correct." The old man's expression clouded with emotion. "He was with a particularly beautiful woman. She must have been about forty years old, and to be quite frank, her clothes were not of the best quality, but she had a full face, her eyes were gentle and yet at the same time very intelligent. She was a very attractive woman.

"Normally, I wouldn't hesitate to go and say hello, but the two of them seemed to be so involved with each other, they seemed to be treasuring every moment they spent together, and I couldn't bring myself to intrude. Even when they left, I kept out of their way and watched them go from the corner of the lobby."

"Thank you very much, that is most interesting," Nakazato said gratefully.

"Oh, dear, what have I done, I didn't mean to talk about the guests like that," the old man suddenly realized.

"Did Okito come by car?"

"Yes, a hired car."

"Do you know which company it was from?"

"Yes, it was from Fuji-Yoshida, their limousines often bring guests here."

"I see, well thank you very much, it's been very interesting talking to you."

Nakazato looked quite excited as he bowed and made his exit. He remembered Inspector Dan telling him that he thought that there was a good chance that the string of murders had been planned by Okito before he died or by someone else, someone close to him, who wanted revenge for his death. The only problem was that the police had not been able to find anyone close enough to Okito to have been willing to commit murder for his sake. . . .

IV

Wednesday, June 17, saw the return of the rainy season and a cold drizzle had been falling since morning.

At three o'clock that afternoon, Akira Takubo drove out of his parents' home in Tsuru city. His parents were both still in their midforties and worked a family farm there. He had a sister, too, who still attended high school; she, too, lived in Tsuru with her parents.

Akira lived on his own in an apartment near his university in Tokyo. He had originally intended to go to a public university, but had not been able to get in and eventually had to wait another year before he finally managed to get into a private one. In his first year, he had spotted an old yellow Mirage in a corner of a used-car dealer's lot and had bought it on impulse. The car cost a lot to run and Akira had to work hard at a hotel and as a teacher at a prep school in order to make ends meet. Despite his busy life, he always managed to find the time to visit his parents once a month.

One reason for this was that when he left, his mother always loaded him down with vegetables, meat, and other things that they produced on the farm, and this helped tide him over until he came for his next visit.

This time he had come to visit the previous Friday, but as he did not have any lectures scheduled at college until Wednesday, he had stayed for a long weekend. He had decided to get back to Tokyo that afternoon and had left early in order to avoid the evening rush hour in Tokyo. As always, he left with the trunk of the car packed with food.

The planting of the rice fields had just concluded and the fields were a beautiful pale green, with streaks of silver running through them where the water shone through the rows. The mountains in the background were cloaked in mist and could not be seen.

Akiro reached Route 139 and turned in the direction of the expressway entrance. Route 139 ran all the way from Otsuki, through Fuji-Yoshida, past the Five Lakes, and down to Fuji city on the Pacific coast, where it joined Route 1.

He wondered if Toko was at the college today and looked up at the heavy clouds overhead. He had been in the college canteen on the tenth when he saw a report on the television about the explosion at the Ruco Corporation. Although he had hurried to find Toko, she had left just before he got to her room. He had waited two days without calling her, guessing that it must be a very difficult time for her, but she did not come to school and finally he telephoned on the evening of the twelfth. Her mother, Sachiko, had answered the phone and told him that Toko was in bed with a cold. Sachiko had always sounded very relaxed when he had called in the past, but this time even she could not hide the tension in her voice, so he soon hung up.

Akiro realized that with Koji's grisly murder, things must be very hectic indeed at Ruco. Toko's father, Hiroshi, was now the most senior executive in the company and no doubt the police and the press were calling at their house, which meant that on top of everything else, they had to answer questions and help with the inquiry. Finally, he realized that Hiroshi would inevitably be the next target on the murderer's list and would have to be on his guard for the next attack.

The whole family must be exhausted, both physically and mentally, and he wondered if he should go and see Toko to cheer her up. Not so long ago, he would have gone without a minute's hesitation, but now . . . now he thought it best to leave her on her own. If she asked for his help, he would do everything he could for her, but until then, he assumed she probably preferred to be on her own.

He had no sooner made up his mind to do so than his thoughts turned to the black Porsche that had appeared outside the coffee shop near the college, with the young arty-looking man inside who had virtually whisked Toko off from under his nose.

Maybe it would be best if he phoned her tonight after he got back to his apartment and found out how her cold was; he hoped it had not gotten any worse.

He drove around a bend and started to accelerate, then suddenly braked again and peered through the windshield.

A black Porsche—yes, he wasn't mistaken, it was identical to the one he had just been thinking about, and there it was, parked at a gas station a little farther down the road. At this point, the road ran parallel to the railway lines and a short distance beyond the gas station, which was surrounded by large billboards, was a sawmill.

Akira drove past the gas station and pulled into the mill; luckily the rain had kept all the workers indoors and nobody came to see what he wanted. He turned the car around and inched out into the road. He could feel his pulse quicken with excitement. As he had driven past, he noticed that the Porsche had Tokyo plates and that a young man was sitting in the driver's seat. It was parked to one side of the drive-in area, as if the driver had tanked up and was about to leave when, for some reason, he decided to stop.

Akira leaned as far out of the car window as possible in an effort to see the other car better. A pile of lumber about twenty yards away partially blocked his view, but luckily the road curved slightly so the wall of the gas station did not stand in his way.

His pulse quickened again. The Porsche's steering wheel was on the left, so he could see the driver quite clearly. He had longish hair, Western features, and though he was too far away for Akira to see clearly, he certainly resembled the man he had met before. Suddenly, despite the rain, the man opened the window and started to tap his fingers on the window frame. Akira guessed that he was waiting for someone and it occurred to him that tapping the window frame as he did was perhaps habitual for him. That day at the university he had nodded slightly and never taken his eyes off Toko as, Akira recalled, he tapped a steady tattoo on the car door.

At that moment a taxi pulled into the station from the direction of Lake Kawaguchi and a woman in a beige raincoat with a dark blue scarf on her head emerged. As if the driver had been waiting for this, the Porsche rolled toward her and the man reached over to open the passenger door.

The woman slipped in and closed the door just as Toko had done that day.

I'm sorry, Akira, Toko had said that day as she sped away from him.

The Porsche soon pulled away, and as it passed him, Akira was able to see the driver quite clearly; no doubt about it, it was Akihito Shirafuji. He could not see the passenger, but as the car passed, he fancied that he heard Toko's voice saying "I'm sorry, Akira."

He pulled out behind them and they continued in the direction he had been going before he stopped. They passed the crossroads outside Tsuru Station and the Porsche headed for the expressway. There were three or four cars in between them, but when they entered the expressway, only one white sedan remained.

The Porsche was heading toward Otsuki and Tokyo. The road was quite empty, and if the other car were to speed up, Akira didn't stand a chance of keeping up with it. Anyway, he guessed that they would be heading back to Tokyo, and if he were to sit right on their tail, Toko would probably notice him and would feel uncomfortable. He need not have worried, however; maybe it was due to the rain, but the Porsche kept its speed down.

They continued in this way for about ten minutes with the white car in the middle until they reached Otsuki, where the road merged with the main one from Kofu and the number of cars increased somewhat. They passed through about five short tunnels until they came to the top of Dango Hill. Akira was surprised at how well his Mirage was running; although he had not done so deliberately, he found that he had been keeping a fixed distance behind the Porsche. He, in turn, was being followed by a small gray car that seemed to be using him as a pacemaker, and they continued in this fashion through the rugged mountains, passing the occasional village huddled in the valleys.

Akira was used to the road and it came as a surprise to him when the black sports car pulled over to the exit lane before the Lake Sagami interchange. So they weren't going straight back to Tokyo after all, they were going to stop off somewhere.

The white car that had been in between him and the Porsche continued straight ahead, but Akira did not cease his pursuit. Now that he knew that the couple were going to stop somewhere, he was determined to find out where and to do so without attracting their attention.

He wondered idly where the woman had come from, but he did not have time to worry about this now; he had to concentrate on following the other car without being seen.

The gray car also followed him off the expressway.

The road proceeded down a hill until it reached the junction with the road that ran along the circumference of the lake. The rain had not slackened at all, and as he drove, Akira was only able to see glimpses of the lake through the gray mist that threatened to obliterate the scenery completely.

Barely visible was a small promontory on the opposite shore, covered with small buildings that he guessed were motels. When he had first purchased this car, he had brought his family here for a drive, but there had not been nearly so many buildings in those days. He spied a huge hotel like a fairy-tale castle in the woods and then came to another one built next to the road, five stories high and built to resemble a battleship.

The Porsche drove across the suspension bridge that spanned the lake and soon turned off onto a small private road leading down a hill. Eventually, Akira was able to make out an old brick building through the trees; he guessed that it was an old resort hotel that had stood here since long before all the motels started to move into the area.

The Porsche stopped in the parking lot in front of the hotel. It was not very large, and only three other cars were parked there. Akira pulled up behind a huge cedar tree and watched to see what they would do next.

The couple got out of the car and walked over the lawn to the main entrance of the hotel, Akihito putting his arm lightly around the woman's shoulders, then they went through the revolving door, one after the other.

Akira drove over to the parking lot and pulled up a short distance from their car. He could not make up his mind whether or not to get out, but having come this far, he could not just go back without doing anything, so he left the car, walked over, and looked through the revolving door.

The lobby was very large, with a grand staircase leading up from the back. A dark red carpet covered the floor, but there was no sign of any guests.

He walked in, and ignoring the man in the dark suit behind the front desk who muttered something to him, he looked quickly around the lobby. There, at the back, below the staircase, he saw an elevator with the door just closing. He caught a glimpse of a woman's beige coat and blue scarf before the door hid her from view.

"Good afternoon, will you be requiring a room?" the man behind the desk asked, but Akira continued to ignore him and walked back out through the revolving door.

He guessed that they would be spending the night in this

hotel and walked off deep in thought, then he stopped in surprise. There was a small gray sedan parked next to his, and as he watched, two men stepped out and started walking toward him. He was sure this was the same car that had been following him on the expressway all the way from Otsuki; it was too unbelievable a coincidence to think that they just happened to decide to stay at this hotel as well.

The two men walked with a strangely confident step. Both wore dark gray suits; one was young and wore glasses—that would be the driver—while the other was a heavily built man in his midforties with a large flat face that looked rather Chinese. The older man threw him a suspicious glance, then continued on to the hotel.

Akira stood and watched as they walked into the lobby and up to the desk, then as he turned back to his car, he remembered something.

He had felt from the moment that he first set eyes on him that he had seen the older man somewhere before, and now he realized that it had been in a magazine. A story about Ryuta's crash had appeared in this issue and accompanying it had been a picture of a man, apparently a policeman, standing staring at the wreckage in dismay.

Under the picture the caption had said, "One of the first people on the scene of the accident was the chief of the Five Lakes police station, Superintendent Ukyo Nakazato, the man who was responsible for solving the case that was known as "The Murder at Mount Fuji."

8

A Trip—Sometime

I

"FRIDAY MAY NINETEENTH," TOKO WHISPERED SOFTLY to herself as she slipped out of bed and stood before the calendar.

The week was finally over and today had arrived at last. Ever since the previous Saturday, when she had met Akihito at the coffee bar in Azabu, she had been counting down the days.

The explosion at the Ruco offices had been on the tenth, and since the morning of the eleventh, her father had been called down to the Marunouchi police station every day for questioning. Toko had been so worried that she had lost her appetite and caught a cold, but then on Saturday, Akihito had called and she had asked him to meet her.

After that Saturday, she had felt as if she were walking on air; she was so tense and excited every day that she could hardly get to sleep until it was almost dawn.

She told herself that he had no right to feel so happy when

there was so much tragedy going on around her and her father was undergoing such a terrible ordeal. At these times, her pain would emerge and the tears would flow all but endlessly.

She had gone to college on Monday and Tuesday, but she had been unable to concentrate on her lectures at all. She had been half-afraid of running into Akira on campus, but she did not see a sign of him and his car was not in the lot, so she guessed he must have gone back to see his parents; he was, she knew, due for a visit.

Wednesday had dawned cold and wet and it brought her cold back. She had a bit of a fever and had stayed in bed until this morning.

The sky was covered in white clouds, but the rain had stopped and there was no wind; it was one of those lovely days that happen every so often during the rainy season when the hydrangeas are at their loveliest. She liked this kind of weather and tonight she would be going on a trip.

"I always like to leave at night when I go on a journey, I find that I can relax better," Akihito had said, and Toko found herself repeating his words to herself several times in the week that followed. "We needn't fix a destination," he had added.

He was going to pick her up in the lobby of the Shiroga-nedai Hotel. He had checked out already in order to concentrate on cleaning up his father's house at Egota, but they had had their first meal together in the restaurant in the hotel's basement and it had a special meaning for them.

At about nine o'clock, Toko came down from her room on the second floor to find her mother in the living room wearing a linen suit.

"Oh, Toko, I was just about to come up and see how you were. How is the cold?" Sachiko asked.

"My temperature has finally gone down," Toko informed her.

"That's good, I must say, you look much better."

"Where is Father?"

"He's gone to the office."

"Don't the police want to see him anymore?"

"They've asked him everything they can think of and there's nothing more they can do. Your father has done nothing to be ashamed of."

Hiroshi's cross-examination had lasted for four days, but the police had at last decided that nothing was to be gained by continuing it any longer and so he was allowed to go straight to the company in the morning.

"That's good," Toko said.

"I was never very worried about your father, but I do wonder how the investigation is going."

"Do you think they have a lead on whoever did it?"

"I have no idea. The press have not been told anything either. The police are doing everything they can to get to the bottom of it, so I should imagine it's just a question of time before we hear something."

"So they still haven't found out who put the poison in our vitamin tablets then?"

"No, it's really frightening, isn't it?" Sachiko frowned and gave a sigh.

The police had asked them repeatedly who had visited the house since the Vitamin E was delivered on March 28, and they had both racked their brains. Nearly all their visitors had been friends and they could not think of a suspicious one in the lot.

"Are you going out?" Toko asked.

"Yes, Hisako is finally going to clean up Ryuta's things at the house in Ogikubo; she phoned me earlier to ask if I could go and help her."

"I see . . . Aunt Hisako must be very lonely on her own."

After Ryuta's death, Hisako had continued to live in the huge blue house. The childless Hisako, like her husband, had looked on Toko almost as her own, and for this reason, Hisako had always felt quite close to Sachiko, too.

"You must go and visit her soon, too," Sachiko told her daughter.

"Yes, I'll do that."

"Are you going to school today?"

"I'm not sure. I've been invited over to Miko's to-night. . . ."

Toko had told her mother that she was going to visit her old high-school friend who had married at the beginning of May; it was one of the few lies she had ever told Sachiko.

"Oh, so you've decided to go then?"

"Yes."

"Well, don't overdo it."

"Don't worry," Toko replied, avoiding her mother's eyes.

Sachiko said that she hoped to be back early that evening and then went out. Toko went up and ran a bath. She generally shampooed her hair every day, but her cold had forced her to break this routine. She usually just had a shower in the mornings, but today she decided to have a bath and get really clean. She soaped herself carefully, and as she did so she felt an excitement building up inside her that she had never felt before.

She finished drying her hair with a blow dryer and was just sitting down to a late breakfast when the phone in the living room rang.

Could it be Akira? she wondered.

She tensed as she picked up the receiver and said hello.

"Toko?"

"Yes . . ."

"It's me, how is it going?"

"Oh, Akira." So, she had been right.

"Is your cold better yet?"

"Yes, just about."

"Oh, will you be coming to school today then?"

Toko looked over at the clock, it was half-past eleven. "It'd be past noon before I could get there and I don't have any important lectures this afternoon, so I think I'll allow myself one more day off."

She did not intend to go the next day either, however.

"I see." Akira was silent for a moment and then he said in formal tone, "I meant to tell you when I saw you next, but I suppose the quicker the better, so I'll tell you over the phone. The police have been following your car. Superintendent Nakazato of the Five Lakes police is on your tail, so be careful.''

"Following us? What do you mean?''

"I don't know either, but I think it would be best if you were to warn Akihito Shirafuji, too, and then act as you think best. That's all, but I mean it, be careful. 'Bye.''

Toko did not know what to say and Akira hung up the phone quietly. She walked back to the table, still not quite sure what to make of Akira's message. No matter how she thought about it, it did not make any sense. She could understand it if the Marunouchi police were following her, given their suspicions about her father, but why the Five Lakes police? And how did Akira happen to get wind of it?

She decided she should get in touch with Akihito and warn him, because even though she herself was baffled by this turn of events, she sensed that Akira had been sincere. It was not just a silly prank; he had told her out of kindness.

It pained her to betray him like this, but she went to the phone and dialed the number of the Egota house. She waited while the phone rang, but there was no answer and she guessed that Akihito must have gone out already.

She put the phone down and went back upstairs to pack. She guessed that they would be spending just one night away, but she could not even be sure of that. She felt a shock of surprise run through her. She did not know where they were going or how long they would stay, and while she guessed that this must be the way that Akihito liked to travel, it frightened her.

She decided to wear a linen jacket and slacks for the trip, but would also pack her favorite floral dress in her shoulder bag.

She was so excited that her chest ached.

At three o'clock, she tried to read a book to force herself to calm down, but her eyes just slid over the words without taking them in. Four o'clock finally passed; she was not due to meet Akihito at the hotel until six, so she still had plenty

of time; it would only take fifteen minutes by taxi from her
house.

She wondered if Sachiko would get back before she left.
This was one of the few times in her life that she wanted to
leave the house without seeing her mother.

What was the weather going to be like? she wondered. It
had been cloudy all day, but would it clear up, or would it
rain? She turned on the radio, but no matter how long she
waited, she heard no forecast. When she finished her preparations, she went downstairs to see if the evening paper had
been delivered. Just as she got to the mailbox, she heard the
sound of the paper being dropped into it.

She took it out and looked at the weather forecast. It predicted a gloomy trend in the Tokyo area and called for rain
during the night, but Toko had no idea where she would be
by then. She turned to the social page and started to look it
over carefully. Ever since Ruco had become news, she had
begun to take more notice of the papers.

In the bottom left corner, she saw a small headline.

WOMAN COMMITS SUICIDE IN LAKE KAWAGUCHI

The name "Kawaguchi" caught her eye and she read on.
Apparently an elderly man had gone fishing in the lake at
seven o'clock that morning and had found a body in about
six feet of water. He contacted the police and they wasted
no time in getting the body out of the water, but the woman
was already dead.

From a notebook found in her handbag, the police were
able to ascertain that the dead woman was Reika Terauchi,
wife of Shohei Terauchi of Lake Kawaguchi town. There was
a short note in the notebook that seemed to indicate that she
had committed suicide and that she had done so that morning, but there was no clue as to her motivation.

Reika . . . in Lake Kawaguchi . . . ? Toko thought,
stunned by the news.

She sat there in shock and Reika's face floated in front of
her eyes, but strangely, it was not the Reika that she had met

at the bar in Fuji-Yoshida the previous month. It was the face of the beautiful woman who had held Okito's hand in Ginza six years ago.

II

She wondered if Akihito had heard about it yet and dialed his number at Egota, but there was still no answer.

She left the house and was hurrying in the direction of Meguro Avenue when she spotted an empty cab and hailed it. It was five past five when she arrived at the Shiroganedai Hotel; she walked through the lobby to a tea room that was situated at the back. The new leaves on the trees outside in the ornamental garden were a beautiful, pale green color.

There was no sign of Akihito yet, so she went and sat down at a table in the corner. The waitress came and she ordered a coffee, but no matter how she tried, she could not suppress the excitement that she felt building inside her.

Why did Reika commit suicide? she thought again and again.

Although it could have been for completely personal reasons, Toko was convinced that it was connected with the Ruco murders somehow. This was pure intuition, but she felt sure that she was right and had a bad feeling about how it would all turn out.

Does Akihito know yet? she wondered.

She wanted to tell him as soon as possible. Although she had no cause, she was very worried; he had not been at the house in Egota since morning. She went out to the lobby and tried his number again, but her call still went unanswered. She returned to her seat to find that her coffee had arrived.

I hope he comes soon, she prayed.

As six o'clock drew nearer, dusk fell and the hotel grew busier as people started to arrive for dinner. Finally, the hands on the clock in the lobby made a single vertical line; it was six o'clock at last, time for their date. Akihito would appear any minute now and she could not wait to see him.

Five past six . . . nine minutes past . . .

"Ah, Akihito!"

She called out quietly to him and rose from her seat as she saw his slim figure coming through the automatic door in the lobby. He was wearing a dark raincoat with the collar turned up and he walked across the carpet directly toward her as if he had known where she was even before he entered the lobby. He came down the steps and entered the tea room, but as he drew closer, Toko realized that it was not Akihito after all. He walked over to another table where there was a young woman waiting and they both started talking happily.

Toko sat down again.

Six-thirteen and the first glimmer of doubt began to creep into her mind. What if he did not come? But that was silly, of course he would come. She bit her lip to hold back the tears she could feel building up inside her and kept her eyes glued to the door.

Some time passed and the door opened again, this time to admit a well-built, middle-aged man. He walked over to the tea room and looked around, then made his way around the tables in her direction.

Toko looked out into the garden. Drops of water left trails along the window glass and she assumed it had started raining again.

Please, hurry up. . . . she begged silently, and turned back to watch the door again. However, her view was blocked by a man's figure standing next to her table. All she could see was a navy blue suit and a white shirt that bulged over an ample stomach. She looked up to see his face and realized that it was the man she had just seen walking toward her. He had a broad, suntanned face, but his eyes were strangely gentle and he looked down at her sympathetically.

"Excuse me, but is your name Toko Chino?" he asked.

"Yes . . . ?"

"My name is Nakazato, of the Five Lakes police."

Toko gave a gasp; Akira had been right, this man had been following her.

"I'm sorry if I gave you a fright, but I'm here tonight because Akihito Shirafuji asked me to come."

"Akihito *asked* you?"

"Yes . . . Would you mind if I sat down?" He pointed at the chair opposite hers.

"Of course not."

He sat down, but he no longer stared at her as he had in the beginning.

"You said Akihito . . . er . . . where is he now?"

"At the Ogikubo police station."

The waitress brought him a glass of water and asked what he would like. He ordered a coffee.

"The Ogikubo police station?" Toko could not understand what he meant. "Since when?" she asked in confusion.

"This morning. We didn't mean to approach him until we'd gotten the whole story from Reika Terauchi, but unfortunately she committed suicide this morning. I can't say how sorry we are that that happened, but it meant that we couldn't waste any time in asking him to come in and help us with our investigation."

"Investigation?"

"I think he knew that we were onto him and he had already written a letter for you before we went to see him. I think that Reika's death was a terrible shock for him."

"Reika and he . . . wha-what is this all about?"

Nakazato did not answer her immediately, he gazed out into the garden, which was now quite dark, for a while before beginning.

"Even though we investigated Okito Shirafuji, we never found even a hint of Reika Terauchi's existence. It was only by chance that we learned he had met her in a hotel by Lake Yamanaka the week before he died."

"Reika and Uncle Okito? When and how did they meet? Please tell me."

Nakazato sat and looked at her in silence for a few minutes.

"One week before he died, on March 17, Okito arrived alone at Kawaguchi Station at three o'clock in the afternoon. He asked the driver of one of the taxis outside to call a limousine and driver for him and then went to Lake Kawaguchi, where he visited a terraced house. He picked up a woman there, and after driving around the lake, they headed for Lake Yamanaka. They drove around the lake for some time, seeming to enjoy the scenery and then they visited a hotel by the lake for an early dinner. The manager of the hotel told me that they seemed to be savoring every moment they were together as if they wanted to remember it forever."

"What happened after that?" Toko demanded, hanging on his words.

"At seven o'clock, they left the hotel in the car he had had wait outside, and after driving her home, he told the driver to take him back to his home at Egota.

"The manager of the hotel knew Okito by sight, but not the woman. However, the driver of the car they used could remember where she lived and we were able to learn that her name was Reika Terauchi. We investigated her background and discovered that her husband was the assistant manager of the Toyo Oil's research laboratory near their house and that she had also worked for the same company before they married. He has been hospitalized for the last six months since he was injured in a traffic accident and she's been working in the lab part-time while he's recuperating.

"That's not all; Toyo Oil makes a lot of products from castor oil and there are always a lot of seeds in the laboratory. Once, one of the staff there made some lysin powder and it was left lying around for a long time."

"So it was Reika who put the lysin in Yaeko's ring," Toko exclaimed. "I suppose she wanted to get revenge for the way Okito was treated."

"No, you've gotten it a little wrong, but I'm sure that it's all written in this letter if you would like to read it."

He took a white envelope out of his suit pocket and put it down on the table in front of her. It was addressed to Toko Chino and signed Akihito Shirafuji on the back in ballpoint pen. The characters looked childlike, as if he were more used to writing English than Japanese.

"But why did he give the letter to you?" Toko asked.

"Ever since we found out about Reika, we kept a watch on her house, and at two-thirty in the afternoon of Wednesday the seventeenth she called a taxi. She was wearing a beige coat and a blue scarf and took the cab to a gas station on Route 139, where there was a black sports car waiting for her."

I bet it was a black Porsche, Toko thought.

"I just happened to have stopped by to see how the surveillance was going when she left the house, so I went along with my men when they followed her. The car left the expressway at Lake Sagami, where the male driver and Reika went into a hotel together and stayed for about two hours. During that time, we were able to get another car ready for when they left.

"At a little after five o'clock a taxi arrived at the hotel for Reika and the man left in the Porsche alone. We also split up, my car following Reika back to her house while one of the men from the station, who is very good at trailing cars, was able to follow the other car back to a house at Egota, and that's how we managed to discover Akihito's identity."

"Is that when you arrested him?" Toko wanted to know.

"No, as I told you just now, we wanted to talk to Reika first. When we had her come into the station yesterday, it really seemed as if she didn't know anything and we let our guard down. We never dreamed that she'd commit suicide the next morning like that." A pained expression came over Nakazato's face and it was a few moments before he could continue.

"As soon as we found out about her death, we contacted

the Ogikubo station and had them hold Akihito. He's suspected of all kinds of things, but we decided it would be quickest if we were to get him to talk to us about the lysin first.

"The interrogation is being done by Inspectors Dan and Wakao, but when I left the station, Akihito told me that you would be waiting here and asked me to give you this letter and . . ."

"What?"

"To tell you that he had really wanted to go away with you, but he had felt all along that he probably wouldn't be able to. He said that he hopes that you'll be able to go on an even better trip one day."

Nakazato's eyes were full of kindness and compassion as he spoke.

III

Dear Toko,

Do you remember, you said that the night before Ryuta died, you saw a dream of my father standing among the storm clouds and you said that people often appear to their loved ones like that around the time that they die?

(As Toko started to read his letter, she felt almost as if Akihito was standing next to her.)

Well, I also saw my father in a dream; it was on March 24 when I was traveling in the countryside in Spain.

In the dream I saw a side of my father that I had never seen before. He said that he hated to have to stop the research he had been working on for the last ten years, his quest to find an alternative source of energy. He was in tears and said that if only he could have a little more time . . . He begged me to come back to Japan and continue his research for him.

Whenever I spoke to him on the phone, he always sounded very bright and told me it would not be long before he succeeded.

When I got back to my house in Paris, I heard he had

died and only just made it back in time for the memorial service a week after his death. Among the mourners, I saw Reika Terauchi. I had seen photographs of her throughout my father's photo albums and read enough about her in my father's diaries to know what she meant to him.

Sometime after my mother's death, he happened to run into her again for the first time since he had taught her at the university, and they gradually grew to love each other. She had gone to work for Toyo Oil immediately after graduation, and although she was still single, my father made no move to marry her, because he knew that he would probably not be able to make her as happy as she deserved to be. He had always been a playboy and he did not want to hurt her.

She understood how he felt and their affair continued for the next ten years, until Shohei Terauchi, a man six years her junior who worked in the same company, proposed to her. My father encouraged her to accept and eventually she did.

You were right; that night you met them in Ginza was their last night together, and although they both intended never to see each other again, this was not to be. They wrote to each other and sometimes my father would go out to Lake Kawaguchi to see her.

I was able to learn all this from reading his letters and diaries, so when I met her at the memorial service, we got together and had a long talk. She reminded me somehow of my mother and she was shocked to see how closely I resembled my father. Fate would not leave us alone and we soon became lovers.

The following Sunday, I drove out to her house at Lake Kawaguchi to see the places that my father had visited with her while he was still alive.

We walked along the lakeside together and she told me that she was working at the laboratory while her husband was in the hospital and we decided to go and see it. I could imagine my father walking with her like this while he was still alive and I felt that he was there with us.

She opened the door and showed me around.

"That is lysin," she happened to mention, pointing to a small bottle of white powder that was lying on one of the shelves, covered in dust. "It's terribly poisonous. One of the staff here extracted it from castor-oil seeds once just to see how it could be done."

There was no reason for her to tell me about it, she just mentioned it in passing, and I wonder now if my father had not been there with us and made her say it. When I left her house that evening, I went back to the laboratory and took the bottle, although I had no idea why.

Ever since I returned to Japan, Yaeko had been trying to get close to me and repeatedly invited me to her home, despite the fact that she seemed to go out of her way to be spiteful to me in public. On the second occasion that I visited her, she asked me into her bedroom, and although I easily avoided her passes, I noticed the cabinet where she kept her rings and the fact that one of the locks on the window was broken and would not shut properly.

On April 28, I heard that she planned to spend the night in Atami, so I broke in, stole her ring, put the lysin in it, made a barb on the inside, and then put it back in her jewelry case before morning. At the same time, I put a fountain pen with my father's name on it under the bed.

Yaeko had originally been my father's mistress, but when things did not go smoothly with his research, she switched to Ryuta and was one of the first to complain when he asked for more money to continue his work. She was an obvious target for revenge, but there was no telling when she might wear the ring or whether the poison would end up in her bloodstream or not. It was a gamble. I was willing to take the chance that things would go as I planned, but I remember thinking that if my father really wanted revenge, he would make sure that it worked.

However, before my plan succeeded or failed, the most

unexpected thing happened. On May 12, Uncle Ryuta's plane crashed and he was killed. What is more, it was rumored that the accident was caused by my father before he died, although we will never know for sure.

I was convinced, though, that Ryuta's "accident" proved that my father wanted revenge, and on the night of his wake, I gave Yaeko a capsule of lysin, telling her that it was a pep pill. The next day she collapsed, and died the day after that. Everyone's attention was focused on the wound on her finger and it was thought that the poison got into her bloodstream from there.

With suspicion growing around my father by leaps and bounds, I purposely left the bottle of lysin in the house at Egota, where it would be found by the police. At the same time, I removed all the photographs of Reika from his albums and hid his diaries and letters. so she would not become the object of a police search.

I had not counted on your intuition, though. When you met my father and Reika in Ginza all those years ago, you instantly realized that she was the woman he loved and you remembered her face ever since. When you asked to look at his albums, I thought that I had removed all the pictures of her, so I was not worried, but you managed to find the only one I missed.

Next, you managed to find out her name, address, and personal history from the university, and you even realized that working for Toyo Oil like that, she could possibly have access to lysin. I cannot tell you how surprised I was when you said that, do you remember? I spoke so loudly that everyone in the coffee bar turned to see what was the matter.

Then you announced that you wanted to go and see her, and since there was no guarantee that you wouldn't go to the police afterward, I decided I would have to remove her presence from your memory. I explained to her what had happened and she agreed to help. She asked her friend who lived next door to tell us the story she did and she

*went to work at the bar for one night only, pretending that
she could hardly even remember that night in Ginza.*

Forgive me, I have tricked you from the beginning.

*I set the bomb that killed Uncle Koji when I went to visit
him at the company after Ryuta died. He had shown me
around the head office and my father's lab when I first
came back—I think he felt a certain degree of responsibility for my father's death and that was why he went to such
lengths to look after me.*

*I learned how to make the nitroglycerine and the timing
device while I was living in America, and several of my
friends in Paris were also interested in that kind of thing.
I bought the ingredients at several shops all over town so
they could not be traced to me.*

*When Koji had shown me around the company the
first time, I carefully noticed its layout, and the second
time I visited I slipped in through one of the open windows to the hall on my way out. I fixed the bomb to the
bottom of the desk where I knew Koji would stand and
then left the same way I entered. It took me less than
five minutes altogether.*

*The first two murders were both made to look as if they
had been done by my father, but my real object lay with
the third attempt.*

*Yes, I am afraid that it was I who put the capsule of
lysin in the bottle at your home. I did it the day we went
to Lake Kawaguchi, when your mother went upstairs to
get us some sweaters and you went into the bathroom to
get ready. I had already heard from you that your parents
took vitamin capsules regularly, but I did not want this
attempt to work; that is why I used a slightly different
capsule and put it at the very bottom, where it would be
found.*

But why did I do it?

*To make the police think that it was not my father
who was responsible for the previous deaths, but yours.
They would think that Hiroshi wanted to become pres-*

ident of the company himself, and that after he had killed the others, he had planted the capsule in his own home in an effort to make it look as if he, too, was a victim.

Do you remember me saying to you that the murderer could have wanted to kill your father, too, and put the blame on my father? When I said that, you mentioned another possibility, that whoever it was wanted to put the blame on your father. Well, you were right again. That is exactly what I wanted.

I just wanted Hiroshi to lose his job. I did not want him to die, and I knew that even if he became a suspect, he would not be proven guilty because the police did not have any real evidence. However, he would never be able to throw off the suspicion that he had killed them and it would stand in his way of becoming the next president. In fact, judging by his character, I guessed that he would resign to save the company from any embarrassment.

When Ryuta died, I inherited a portion of his stock in the company. He originally owned thirty percent of the stock and managed to keep most of my father's stock for himself, which meant that all in all, he owned nearly fifty percent. Since he did not have any children, he left it all to his wife and two brothers, and I was able to inherit my father's share.

When Koji died, he left his stock to his wife and two daughters, but neither Hisako nor Koji's family had any interest in running the company, they only held the stock for its financial value. If I could get Hiroshi out of the way, I then stood a chance of coming out on top and taking over the company.

By so doing, I would not only be able to have revenge for my father, but I could also hire a team of young experts to continue his project. I felt that this was what he wanted me to do when he appeared to me in a dream after he died his lonely death.

But it's funny, isn't it? I had no sooner nearly reached

my goal than it suddenly no longer appeared so attractive.
I am not a brilliant scientist like my father or even a clever
business man like Ryuta. I had obtained revenge for my
father's death and I hoped that he would be happy with
that. I decided to go back to Paris and live there; I feel
more at home there than I do here, and that is why I met
Reika again, to say good-bye.

I knew that I should not meet her again after I stole the
lysin. If anyone realized our relationship, or knew who
she was, it would not be long before they realized where
the lysin had come from and suspicion might even fall on
her. However, I felt that I could not go away without seeing
her just one more time.

Of course I took precautions against being followed. I
had her come and meet me at a garage in Tsuru city and
then we went to an old hotel by Lake Sagami. Unfortunately, this was a fatal mistake. I realized that I was being
followed on my way back to Tokyo, and although I lost the
other car, they had my license plate number, and anyway,
I knew that Reika's taxi would be followed, too.

This morning I was awakened at six o'clock by a
telephone call from Reika. She said that she was just
calling to say good-bye once more, and even though I
guessed what she was about to do, I was powerless to
stop her.

I must stress again that she had nothing to do with any
of this, but it was due to my meeting her that I was able
to steal the lysin and she knew what I had done with it
after that. She was scared that she would be interrogated
by the police, that they would realize where the lysin came
from, and at the last I think that was why she decided to
end things as she did.

It is only a question of time now until the police come
for me.

I really wanted to go for a farewell trip with you, but I
felt all along that it would not be possible and it is probably best this way. I am very pleased that I was able to

meet you, though, and I hope that you will have a wonderful trip someday.

                                        All my love,
                                        Akihito Shirafuji

Toko reread the letter several times, and as she did so, a memory from her past again rose in front of her eyes.

She remembered the sand castle the young boy had helped her build when she was in kindergarten, and how delighted she had been as the turret and castle gate took shape beneath his hands. And she remembered how, when the castle was almost completed, the little boy had smashed it to the ground, as if he had planned to do so from the very beginning, and then walked into the house without a backward glance.

Even now she could picture his straight figure with his long legs protruding from his short trousers as he walked away, further and further into the distance.

About a week later, Toko went to the university for the first time since the conclusion of the case. It was hard to believe that they were still in the rainy season; there was a beautiful blue sky overhead as she walked up the hill to the campus and a small plane flew overhead. It turned and disappeared into the distant clouds.

There's a beautiful clear sky today and very little wind, perfect weather for a flight. She could hear Ryuta's familiar voice in her ear again. *Well, I must be going now; you never know, I might meet Okito on top of the clouds.*

It had all started that day. She felt as if she had already made the trip Akihito had wished for her, a journey that started the day of Uncle Ryuta's death, and she wondered if she really would ever go on another one.

She stopped in front of the notice board next to the office when she heard a voice.

"Toko . . . Toko!"

She looked up to see a tall silhouette running down the

corridor toward her. It was Akira, wearing a striped shirt and jeans, running in his own peculiar way.

"Hey, Toko, long time no see! How's it going?"

"Fine, and you?"

"Great." He nodded and then frowned and stared closely at her. "You've changed, you know."

"Really?"

"Yep, you've definitely changed."

"In what way?"

"I'm not quite sure how to put it . . ." Akira said, smiling widely, "but you're much more attractive than you used to be."

About the Author

The bestselling mystery writer in Japan, Shizuko Natsuki has written over eighty novels, short stories, and serials, forty of which have been made into Japanese television movies. Several of her short stories have been published in *Ellery Queen's Mystery Magazine*. She is also the author of *Murder at Mt. Fuji, The Third Lady, The Obituary Arrives at Two O'clock, Innocent Journey*, and *Portal of the Wind*. Ms. Natsuki lives in Fukuoka, Japan.